Never Run

Richard Stoll

© Richard Stoll 2021

All rights reserved

Distributed by Lulu Press Inc.

(www.lulu.com)

ISBN: 978 - 1 - 008 - 90700 - 3

Preface:

This small volume contains two romantic tales set against the backdrop of the increasingly popular activity of trail running. In both, two young enthusiasts meet unexpectedly and agree to experience the pleasure of mountain running together. To their surprise, they also find love and discover some of the mysteries and wonders of the Christian faith.

Part 1 is a simple romance that takes place in the stunning surroundings of the Swiss Alps. Part 2 is slightly longer and delves more deeply into the past experiences and present emotions of those involved. It begins in England before moving north over the Scottish border and on up the northern half of the West Highland Way – a wildly beautiful hiking trail – before ending in the legendary Isle of Skye.

Cover picture:

The Old Man of Storr – a tall pinnacle of rock on the seaward side of a large group of jaggy outcrops overlooking the east coast of the Island of Skye. The water in the middle distance is Loch Leathan. The sea lies beyond with the island of Raasay and the Scottish mainland fading into the distance.

NEVER RUN ALONE (Part 1)
Chapter 1: Surprise Invitation

At this early hour, the modest dining room was empty except for a young woman sitting at one of three small tables beside a picture window overlooking the village of Lauterbrunnen in the Swiss Alps. The remaining tables had been pushed together in the centre of the room, presumably ready for a large party of guests.

David paused just inside the entrance, wondering where he should sit. Having arrived late the previous evening, this was his first morning – indeed first time – in Switzerland. He was, therefore, both excited and hungry and hoping for more than what his grandparents, based on their experience of nearly fifty years ago, had predicted would be a "continental" breakfast consisting of coffee, white rolls, butter and jam.

To his relief, the self-service table was loaded with plenty of other good things, amongst which were a selection of fruit juices, cereals, yogurt, and slices of ham and cheese. There was even a cauldron of near-boiling water beside a basket of brown eggs.

"That's splendid; some decent food before a day's trail-running," he thought.

At that moment a waitress bustled in with a pot of coffee. Seeing David she said: "Guten Morgen, mein Herr!" Then, realizing he must be the new British guest, she took a deep breath and launched into a laboured explanation in English.

"Hotel Silberhorn did not have enough rooms for a large coach party and some guests had to be transferred to us. They will be using the big table. Two of the small tables are needed by other guests and so I hope you will not mind sharing with the young lady here ..."

She trailed off uncertainly and led David to the chair opposite the young woman who was just finishing a mixture of yogurt and prunes. She had an attractive face and looked remarkably young at close quarters, barely out of her teens, but she nodded pleasantly to David and quietly thanked the waitress for the coffee.

"Tea or coffee, sir?" the waitress asked. "Tea please," David said as he sat down.

Waiting for a moment until the waitress was out of earshot, the girl leaned forward to whisper conspiratorially: "I didn't have time to warn you that the tea will come in a glass with a teabag dangling in water well below boiling. I had it yesterday on my first morning here. It may not be too bad if you like it weak without milk, but the only milk available is that rich full cream stuff on the table over there.... Anyway, you'd better collect your food before the vultures arrive. I'll come with you and rescue my egg."

The girl stood up. She had a strong lithe body and looked extremely fit. As David followed her to the buffet table he was impressed by her smooth athletic strides. After collecting her egg from its small cradle in the cauldron, she cut a thick slice of wholemeal bread from one of the loaves on offer and left him.

After gingerly putting his egg in one of the colour-coded cradles, David selected the rest of his breakfast. By the time he was seated again, his glass of tea had arrived and the girl was staring rather forlornly at the egg yolk dribbling down the outside of the shell.

"I didn't leave it in long enough! There's a notice saying that for a firm egg you need to leave it for eight minutes."

David nodded. "It's the altitude," he explained. "Lauterbrunnen is 800m above sea level and so water boils at about 97°C. The cauldron is probably even lower to prevent the water boiling away too quickly."

The girl looked impressed. "I guess you've been to university and studied science?"

"I've just graduated in Physics at Durham University, or at least I will have after the graduation ceremony at the end of

July," David admitted. "My parents and several other relatives have clubbed together to pay for this 10-night Swiss holiday because they know I'm addicted to trail running; it's a sort of congratulations prize."

He suddenly felt embarrassed to have revealed so much to a stranger, but she was remarkably easy to talk to. "Running in the mountains will be a wonderful way to unwind as well as being splendid exercise," he ended.

The girl's eyes lit up. "That's amazing! I live in Bishop Auckland, just over ten miles southwest of Durham," she exclaimed in surprise, adding, even more enthusiastically, "and I love real trail running. Unfortunately, that means a cycle ride of at least twenty miles to find any decent slopes."

It occurred to David that she must be tough if she could happily fit all that cycling and goodness knows how much running into one day, but all he said was: "I'm David, by the way."

"Joanna, but I prefer Jo," the girl said. She gave him a friendly smile.

They continued eating in comfortable silence for a few minutes and then Jo spoke again.

"Yesterday, I ran four miles south up the valley to a hamlet called Stechelberg and then jogged up a steep path to Mürren on the cliff top, a climb of at least 800m. I certainly needed a refreshment break when I got there! The views from the café terrace were superb. Afterwards, I came back along the top of the cliff to the cable station above Lauterbrunnen and scrambled down another path."

She paused and looked across the table at David. "Today, I'm planning to go up to Kleine Scheidegg, the top of the pass between here and Grindelwald, a climb of 1250m over a distance of about six and a half miles. I hope to be able to run – or at least jog – most of the way there and back. Would you like to join me?" She smiled invitingly.

"I'd love to come if you're sure I won't be in the way. This is my first time at high altitude."

Jo grinned, clearly pleased. "It's only my second time and we can take it fairly easily with a short break in Wengen, nearly 500m up the side of the valley, and again at Wengernalp, another 600m higher," she said. "Shall we meet in forty minutes outside the hotel entrance? I'll bring my map of the area. Don't forget to do a few warm up exercises first and bring plenty of water and your sun cream."

......

David was waiting when Jo emerged from the shadow of the hotel doorway into the bright sunlight.

He had difficulty suppressing a gasp: in all his admittedly limited experience, he had never seen such a vision of athleticism. Wearing navy-blue running shorts and a sleeveless white tank-top, Jo looked more than ready for any challenge. The first garment did little to conceal perfectly muscled legs and the second was short enough to allow his admiring eyes to appreciate washboard abs that would have been the envy of most bodybuilders. Not least, the delightful face that had looked at him across the breakfast table was smiling gently as if (was it really possible?) she was also pleased with what she was seeing.

All she said, however, was: "Ready? Then follow me," before leading him down through the station subway and past a multi-storey car park used by visitors taking the narrow gauge cog-railway up to Wengen and Kleine Scheidegg.

They soon reached a path that began to wind its way up the eastern side of the valley, but it was only when the gradient became really steep that Jo slowed to a jog or even, very occasionally, a brisk climb.

"If this is what she calls taking it "fairly easily" then it's a good job I'm fit!" David thought as he followed her relentless progress. "I can't let this amazing girl, however tough, show me up."

Nevertheless, he was relieved when she paused for a drink and there was an opportunity to gaze back into the valley below them, its depth accentuated by the long Staubbach waterfall cascading down the cliff face on the far side of Lauterbrunnen. Two pairs of eyes were then almost automatically drawn south down the long deep trough to the valley's end, beyond which three mountains soared up to meet the pale blue sky. The central peak resembled a snow-covered pyramid.

"Aren't they splendid?" Jo remarked. "The one in the middle is the Breithorn. It's not quite as high as the Jungfrau that will tower above us as we approach Kleine Scheidegg."

The three mountains did indeed form a beautiful backdrop but David was even more intrigued by the girl beside him. "I'm sorry, but I can't help admiring your abs!" he said rather diffidently. "I regularly do the plank – 60 seconds up followed by 15 seconds down for about ten minutes – but mine are not nearly as good as yours!" He shyly lifted his running vest for a second.

Jo grinned. "Well, you've been a hard-working student for the last few years whereas I'm on the ground maintenance team at our local golf course. It's hard work and I'm often out in all weathers, which certainly toughens me up! Of course, I'm not yet allowed anywhere near the greens; they're the preserve of the green-keepers! I'm also a member of a local gym."

......

The young couple jogged on and, after one more brief stop, reached the outskirts of Wengen and a surprisingly steep road that climbed up under the railway and out on to a small level area beside the station where benches had been placed for the benefit of visitors. Sitting down gratefully, Jo produced a banana, opened one end and offered half to her companion. "We need to keep up our minerals etc.," she said.

There was a brief hoot and an up-bound train consisting of bright yellow and green carriages slowly rumbled into the station. Quite a lot of people alighted and a few got on, but the train still looked uncomfortably full.

"I hope the café in Kleine Scheidegg is not too busy," David remarked.

Jo shook her head. "Most people going up there at this time of day are aiming even higher; a cog railway climbs from there to Jungfraujoch, a famous sightseeing spot on the saddle between the Mönch and the Jungrau. The trip is very expensive and certainly too much for me!"

She paused to put the banana skin in a nearby rubbish bin. Then standing beside David, who was still seated and making the most of the short rest, she shouldered her rucksack to announce: "Having climbed roughly 500m in a north-easterly direction to get here, we now have to go south for over three miles along the side of the valley, climbing nearly all the time until we get to Wengernalp. After that the path gradually veers northeast and goes up another couple of hundred metres to Kleine Scheidegg."

As she spoke, her eyes lit up at the thought of testing her legs and lungs on the climb ahead. Her enthusiasm was so infectious that David sprang to his feet. He normally preferred to run alone, not only liking the freedom and solitude, but also not wanting to be held up by a companion who preferred a slower pace. However, there seemed to be no likelihood of this girl running too slowly; in fact it might well be the reverse!

......

After crossing the railway track a short distance above the station, Jo led the way up a narrow road that climbed through the outskirts of the village. A tantalising glimpse of the western edge of the Jungfrau appeared beyond the end of a ridge now rising steeply not far to the left of the road.

Before long, they emerged on more open ground. The cliffs and mountains on the other side of the Lauterbrunnen valley were in full view again, although the bottom was out of sight. It was now apparent that Wengen sat on a shelf or terrace partway up the eastern side of the valley and that this terrace gradually widened as it tilted up towards the Jungfrau.

The scene so captivated David that he let out a loud shout of appreciation. Jo waved happily in response. It was then that the realization hit him; he was not merely enjoying running with her, it was a sheer delight.

The cog railway to Kleine Scheidegg was never far away, as evidenced by occasional glimpses of the track or rumble of a train, and so the young couple were not surprised when their route led them past a small station signposted as Allmend. The lane had reduced to a gravel track by now but was still easy to run on, even though it frequently climbed steeply as it wound its way over sunlit meadows and past thickets of conifer trees.

......

As she led David onwards and upwards through such a splendid setting, Jo began to process all that had happened since he had suddenly appeared at her breakfast table. Although she was friendly by nature, her readiness to be as helpful as possible had surprised her because she was usually rather cautious when it came to the opposite sex. In fact, her friends often teased her that she was much more interested in running than in boyfriends. Yet today she had not only given away much more information about herself and her plans than polite conversation demanded but even gone on to invite David to accompany her. Was it purely on the basis of his enthusiasm for trail running? Somehow she did not think so. In fact, she now felt slightly ashamed she had led the initial climb up to Wengen at such a brisk pace after promising to take his first high altitude run fairly easily. However, she had certainly been impressed by the fact that he had not asked her to slow down.

As she pondered further on their unexpected encounter, she suddenly recalled that, since becoming a Christian a few years before, she had frequently asked God to reveal more of his plan for her life. Perhaps this beautiful morning in these wonderful surroundings would turn out to be one of those times? Excitement filled her and she surged onwards with renewed energy.

......

Later, after another brief stop for water, the two runners entered a much larger wood. The track snaked through densely packed trees for a surprising distance before the trees began to yield to patches of open ground again, providing delightful hints of the beauty to come.

Eventually, after climbing nearly 500m above Wengen, the path levelled off and began to turn as it neared the end of the ridge. Suddenly Jo, with David hard on her heels, rounded a bend and they were completely out in the open.

They stopped to gaze in wonder. The scene before them was breathtaking. Not far beyond the ridge, the mighty Jungfrau and its satellite peaks soared skywards.

"It was worth coming all the way to Switzerland just to see this!" Jo cried.

Neither of them had experienced anything so awe inspiring; this was a place where anything might happen.

After a moment of dazed silence, David turned to say something, but the words froze on his lips. Even the proximity of the great mountain had suddenly faded into relative insignificance. All that really mattered was the radiant girl beside him and it was no longer just because she had a delightful face and beautiful athletic figure. He too now found himself struggling to analyse his feelings.

At breakfast, Jo had been remarkably friendly and so obviously a fellow enthusiast that he had readily accepted her invitation to join her on the day's outing. Admittedly, she had looked stunning in her running gear and his admiration had continued to grow during the tough climb, but now something far stronger had come into play. It was not merely sexual attraction he was experiencing; but what was it? Then he had the glimmer of an idea. But first it was high time to say something reasonably sane.

"The Jungfrau certainly is a fabulous sight, especially covered in so much snow," he agreed, "but I must say that sharing it with you makes it far better!"

They smiled at each other uncertainly and then Jo, to give herself time to process this last remark, suggested they sat on a nearby seat strategically placed to enjoy the view. Once settled, David glanced cautiously sideways only to see that she appeared to be totally absorbed in the marvellous scene. Sensing his glance, however, she turned to meet his gaze.

Their eyes locked and, in some mysterious way, both knew that something very special was happening.

It was Jo who broke the ensuing silence. "You're a Christian, aren't you? I've been one since I was sixteen."

Strangely, David was not taken by surprise; it was as if, deep down, he had been expecting it.

"For me, it was during my second year at university. A friend lent me a book when I was in bed with 'flu," he said slowly. "It all happened very quickly."

"We must tell each other about our experiences later," Jo replied with a delighted smile, "but now we ought to get going again. Would you like to lead this time? Wengernalp station should be just ahead and then Kleine Scheidegg is slightly over a mile further."

David returned her smile and set off at a smart trot, his heart almost bursting with emotion but also eager to see what would unfold as the path continued to round the end of the ridge.

The railway line appeared below them and, not far beyond, the terrain sloped down for a short distance before disappearing abruptly into what appeared to be a chasm. As the path continued to curve east, more and more of the mountain range emerged. First the Mönch and, finally, the last of the famous three: the Eiger. The sight was more than enough to make David slow to a walk to give them time to take it in.

It was a few seconds before they realised that they could also see another mountain just to the west of the Jungfrau. It was considerably lower and formed the end of the formidable range. In fact, its western edge appeared to drop down so sharply into the Lauterbrunnen valley that it gave the impression of having been chiselled off by a giant stonemason.

David speeded up again and led Jo gradually down until they were running alongside the railway. Then the path dropped behind the small Wengernalp station building before climbing again to pass the terrace of a surprisingly large hotel. "Hotel Jungfrau" was displayed on its shuttered facade. Being relatively early in the summer season, it was still closed.

Leaving the hotel behind, the path turned sharp right and passed under the railway before turning back to continue east. The young couple found they were now heading directly towards the Eiger and crossing a steeply sloping meadow covered in a profusion of alpine flowers that trembled in the delicious breeze. Several small buildings were dotted around, presumably for the care of cows when in high alpine pasture.

By now the path had become a nicely gravelled track again and Jo moved up to run alongside David, much to his pleasure. It felt wonderful to be running so close to her through such a wonderful landscape. There were more hikers around and he surmised that some had probably taken the train to Kleine Scheidegg and were walking the modest distance to Wengernalp and back. Every so often he had to move over on to the grass to allow them to pass.

It was not long before the track headed in a more northerly direction, as evidenced by the fact that the Eiger was now further to their right, and climbed more steeply. Even Jo seemed happy to slow to a jog. Then some buildings appeared on the horizon; they were approaching their destination.

CHAPTER 2: The Trümmelbach Falls

"This is really good soup!" Jo declared.

She and David were seated at one of the long tables on the terrace of the station café in Kleine Scheidegg. A short distance away the little red carriages of a Jungfraujoch train were filling up with tourists eagerly looking forward to the trip ahead.

"Yes, it certainly is, and well worth the wait," her companion replied. It was the height of the lunch period and the café was busy.

"We needed a rest anyway," Jo said, "and some people would pay a fortune to be looking at a view like this!"

She was right. The vast expanse of the Eiger, Mönch and Jungfrau towered above them, making the little red train slowly threading its way back down the snow-covered slope look totally puny. Picking up another piece of wholemeal bread and chewing it slowly, she examined her map. After a short pause, she looked up with a smile.

"Just before we get to Wengernalp, I think I've spotted another way to get back to Lauterbrunnen," she said. "It'll mean a zigzag descent down a very steep path that comes out near the bottom of the Trümmelbach Falls, about two miles south of the village."

"It sounds brilliant and will really test our thighs!" David replied.

......

After a quick visit to the surprisingly clean station toilets, the young couple walked back past the main railway tracks to reach the Wengernalp path. No less than three trains were waiting to depart. Only then did they realise that the lines coming up from Lauterbrunnen and Grindelwald respectively were separate and anyone wishing to travel between the two places had to change at Kleine Scheidegg.

"That explains why there are so many tracks on this side of the station building," David commented.

"I suppose most travellers are aiming to hike in this vicinity or join the Jungfraujoch railway on the other side of the station," Jo added.

David nodded. "Yes; if you just want to get from one village to the other there's a quicker and cheaper route via Zweilütschinen – the junction where the train from Interlaken divides in two and vice-versa."

They ran on happily down the long winding trail until, not far from the Hotel Jungfrau, Jo called a halt. "That was a splendid, if easy, run in delicious mountain air," she enthused, taking a drink from one of her recently replenished flasks before consulting the map.

Just ahead, the route to Wengernalp turned sharp right to go under the railway line, but, immediately on their left, a narrow path meandered south across a steep meadow. Jo folded the map again and pointed. "We go this way," she said and bounded off exuberantly.

David followed, admiring her sure-footedness on the uneven surface. The path soon took them below the tree line and into an increasingly dense wood before merging with a wider track running east-west. Here they ran abreast for several minutes before pausing to get their bearings.

The trees had thinned considerably again, revealing a splendid view to the left over the tops of conifers now clinging precariously to what remained of the slope before it plunged out of sight. The mountains in the background looked familiar.

"Why, that's the western end of the Jungfrau range. I was expecting to see the far side of Lauterbrunnen valley!" David said in surprise.

"Below us is the narrow Trümmelbach valley: a deep gorge the river has cut into the rock," Jo explained. "We should soon come to another path on our left that will go down into it."

She grinned at him, relishing what was to come. He beamed back, loving every minute of this adventure with such a companion and followed her onwards.

The trees became even less frequent and it was not long before they were out in the open under the bright afternoon sun and surrounded by glorious alpine scenery. The excellent track was descending steeply now and frequently formed a long loop intended to lessen the gradient. However, a generation of eager hikers had worn shortcuts to save time and these Jo used with her customary verve.

It was not long before it became apparent that the track had turned in a more northerly direction parallel to the main valley. The village of Mürren could be seen on the far side and appeared to be on roughly the same level as the runners.

"I must take you there one day," Jo called out, just before spotting a tall post beside the track bearing several yellow direction signs. The first indicated that the main track led to Allmend and Wengen, and a second pointed down a narrow path on the left.

"This is the path I was looking for!" she exclaimed with relief. "I was beginning to think I'd missed it."

......

The young couple followed the winding path down the slope, dodging in and out of small clumps of trees. By now they had become accustomed to paths that frequently dipped, twisted and turned, but this was their first experience of one that did it to such an extent that they felt quite disorientated.

"Anyway we're making good time and the scenery is brilliant," Jo called over her shoulder as she reduced her pace.

However, it was not long after threading their way across yet another small meadow that they found themselves zigzagging down a path that appeared to cling to the side of the slope almost as desperately as the surrounding conifers. Great care was essential to avoid tripping over the profusion of tree roots and rocks, but this did not dampen their enthusiasm in the least.

A moment of awe came when the young couple caught their first glimpse of the foaming Trümmelbach surging down the narrow channel that the water had gradually worn through the rock. A very descriptive pictorial sign beside the path made it clear that the channel must be crossed quickly.

"Apparently there's sometimes a sudden surge of melt water if a lump of the glacier has broken off," David said, reading the warning written in no less than three languages.

But Jo was more interested in what water power can do over the ages. "Not far below us the Trümmelbach has carved its way down inside the cliff, forming a series of falls that tourists can pay to see," she informed her companion. "Unlike the other waterfalls for which the Lauterbrunnen valley is famous, the only sign of water at the bottom is a stream running out from the base of the cliff to join the main river – the Lütschine."

Reluctantly they moved on. Whilst still amongst the trees, the path was very similar to before, but, nearer the bottom, it became a series of rough-hewn steps so steep and narrow that a stout safety cable had been attached to the adjacent cliff face as an aid for hikers. Although Jo and David were now much closer to the bottom, the views were still superb, especially of the village not far to the north.

"Lauterbrunnen may look close but it's still about one and a half miles as the crow flies," Jo remarked at one point.

So it was that, an hour after leaving Wengernalp, the young couple reached the bottom, crossed a small meadow and emerged on a road. Here Jo took out her map before turning right and leading David past the Trümmelbach Visitor Centre. A hundred yards or so later, she found a path leading off to the left that took them across the Lütschine to join a wide pedestrian path.

"This is the route from Lauterbrunnen to Stechelberg that I followed yesterday morning before climbing up to Mürren. It saves hikers having to use the road," she explained.

They jogged on happily and arrived back at the hotel a few minutes after four o'clock. As they were collecting their keys, David said: "May I invite you to coffee and cake? There's a café about two minutes away near the station."

"Thanks, I'd love some!" Jo replied warmly. "See you down here in ten minutes."

......

The slice of cake Jo chose was so generous that she asked David if he would share it. "I must watch my sugar intake," she said.

The girl behind the counter clearly understood her comment because she smiled understandingly and offered to provide an extra cake fork. So it was that the young couple were soon sipping excellent cups of coffee and tucking into a delicious cake.

"You've given yourself the smaller piece," David objected. "After all that exercise, you must have burnt a good few calories. Anyway, you certainly don't need to worry about your figure – it's perfect!"

Jo blushed, obviously pleased with the compliment but not wanting to pursue the topic. "You're bigger than I am. Anyway, I don't want to spoil the evening meal; it was good last night."

After a pause, she added: "I expect you know that small Swiss hotels have a fixed menu in the evening; it obviously saves money because there's less food wasted. You can always ask what the main course will be at breakfast time and order an omelette or something instead."

"I'm happy with most things. There was no choice at college either," David told her. "By the way, this coffee and cake has not replaced my earlier invitation to come out for a drink after dinner!"

Jo looked at him in a way that made his heart beat faster. "I'm looking forward to it! However, in future I'm going to pay my share."

"We'll argue about that another time!" he replied firmly.

......

David knocked on Jo's bedroom door at six forty-five prompt. She must have been waiting for him because the door opened within seconds. Freshly showered and hair washed, she was wearing an attractive cornflower blue top with long sleeves.

"Sorry it's a bit creased," she apologised.

"You look fantastic; heads are going to turn downstairs!" David whispered, giving her a quick kiss on the cheek. "Anyway the creases match the ones in my shirt!"

Jo grinned and took his hand as they descended the stairs. "I'm hungry and glad the Swiss like to eat early," she said.

David chuckled. "Two years ago, a student friend and I went backpacking in Greece. One evening we went to a small restaurant at seven o'clock hoping to get a meal. The door was open and a waiter was laying up the tables but he looked at us in astonishment when he realized we wanted something to eat. Gesturing to a clock on the wall, he managed to make it clear we were well over an hour early!"

......

The large central table in the dining room had been split up into its smaller segments. The coach party had obviously departed and were many miles away by now.

The waitress was the same as at breakfast. She smiled conspiratorially when David indicated that he wanted to sit with Jo, but all she said was, "I hope you had a good day," as she left them with the menu.

Jo had been right: there was no choice. Although the menu was in German, a brief English translation had been added below each item; vegetable soup would be followed by braised beef with sauté potatoes and a side salad, and, to finish, apricot desert. The management, keen to increase their alcohol sales, had also listed three recommended wines. The first was a Swiss red wine and it was the only one available by the glass.

"Would you like a glass of wine?" David asked his companion. "It might go quite well with the beef, not that I know much about wine."

"I'd love to try a little but I think a whole glass will be too much," Jo said. She had already noticed the generous size of the glasses on a neighbouring table.

Fortunately, the waitress had overheard this remark when bringing the soup. "If you have a bottle you can help yourself to what you want. I'll write the table number on the bottle and put it out every evening."

"Then we'll have a bottle of your recommended Swiss red, please," David said.

"But charge it to my room: number 203," Jo interjected before David could give his own. He tried to object after the waitress had left, but Jo insisted.

"I want to pay my fair share of the extras we'll be buying over the next few days and you've already paid for several things today," she said.

For people not accustomed to the niceties of wine, the relatively low-alcohol wine turned out to be a pleasant accompaniment to the main course.

All in all, David's first dinner with Jo was a great success; not only did they feel just as happy together as they had done earlier in the day but somehow the wine added something extra. Jo summed it up when she commented, just before the apricot desert arrived: "Wine, even just a little, makes a meal extra special!"

She was too shy to add that David's presence made it even more special.

......

After the meal, they strolled arm-in-arm down the village street and found a café for a hot drink before continuing south as far as the Staubbach waterfall. They had only paused briefly on the way back that afternoon but now walked up the narrow approach path until within reach of spray carried on the gentle gusts of wind.

Without a word, David bent over towards Jo, her smiling face just visible in the fading light. A moment later, they shared their first kiss.

"Just think," he whispered. "If I had gone to some other hotel or, even worse, some other village, I would never have met you!" He sounded appalled at the thought.

But Jo smiled confidently. "It was all part of God's plan," she replied. "I simply selected Lauterbrunnen because it looked like a convenient place from which to run without needing to use expensive public transport too often. I was also looking for a modest hotel with good reviews."

David chuckled. "It was the same for me. Anyway, the place we're in is comfortable, the shower works and the meal tonight was excellent."

"Even better than last night, although I'm probably a bit biased!" Jo added impishly.

With that David swung her round and kissed her properly, marvelling at the feel of her firm body pressed against his. Her lips, however, were anything but firm. It was at least five minutes before they strolled slowly back to the hotel and parted reluctantly outside Jo's bedroom door.

CHAPTER 3: Grindelwald

The weather the following morning was not nearly as good as on the day before and the mountains were shrouded in cloud. However, Jo and David were heartened when the waitress informed them that the forecast was better for later in the day.

David had a suggestion. "Suppose we climb up to Kleine Scheidegg using the route we returned by yesterday and then run the six miles or so down into Grindelwald. After a light meal there and depending on how we feel, we could then either get the train back here via Zweilütschinen or run back to Scheidegg and take the train down through Wengen."

Jo nodded enthusiastically. "Good suggestion! It would also be nice to spend time in Grindelwald; it's said to be a lovely village. Hopefully the mountains will have cleared by then."

As it turned out, the clouds had already begun to lift by the time they set out at eight-thirty. David took them swiftly south as far as the foot of the Trümmelbach Falls and then left Jo to lead the climb. Such was her enthusiasm, aided by the delicious air, that it did not seem long before the gradient eased and her brisk climb turned into a steady jog.

......

The young couple had a breather at the point where the path from the valley joined the main track near Wengernalp before setting off on the gradual climb to Kleine Scheidegg. They were looking forward to a refreshment stop on the terrace outside the station café but it turned out to be even busier than the day before.

"Never mind," David said. "There's a café in Alpiglen, roughly three miles down towards Grindelwald. Apparently it has a terrace overlooking the valley."

"I'm game if you are," Jo said. "If we just have water now, a coffee break will be all the nicer later, especially as the clouds are still lifting and the sun is showing signs of breaking through."

Thus, after a short stop, they moved on, eager to see what lay in the next valley. David wondered if it was just his imagination or was the snowline lower here than it had been on the Lauterbrunnen side; certainly it was still surprisingly thick on the slope not far above them and there were frequent trickles of melt water crossing the path. Meanwhile, Jo delighted in the profusion of small alpine plants not long freed from their winter captivity.

......

It was impossible to miss the café in Alpiglen because the path ran directly through its garden. The terrace was fairly busy but the young couple managed to find a table near the balustrade with a view of the valley and Grindelwald nestling far below. The clouds were continuing to disperse and most of the Eiger was visible to their right; even better, the Wetterhorn stood proud and graceful not far beyond.

"Wonderful!" Jo whispered. "It was a brilliant idea to come here." The smile she gave David warmed his heart.

"This must be the second-best view we've had, only surpassed by our first sight of the Jungfrau at close quarters yesterday," he agreed.

"The coffee is good as well," Jo said happily.

......

As the path snaked its way downwards, the beautiful Wetterhorn kept coming into direct view giving Jo a strange sense of elation. "I suppose it's a natural response to seeing such beauty in God's creation," she thought.

The cog-railway was never far away and, about a mile later, they passed Brandegg station and another café-restaurant – still closed so early in the summer season. The rest of the splendid run covered almost three miles surprisingly quickly as the route, now occasionally a well-constructed road, continued down the slope. They crossed a fast flowing river at the bottom only to be confronted by a steep climb to the village centre.

A few strenuous minutes later they came out beside Grindelwald Dorf station at the lower end of Dorfstrasse. It was clear this was the main street, filled as it was by shops, cafés and hotels. In the distance, framed by buildings on either side of the road, towered the rather threatening north face of the Eiger, its image only softened by the snow at the top.

"No wonder the north face of the Eiger is so difficult to climb: it's almost vertical!" David exclaimed as he took Jo's elbow and guided her towards a café. "Now for some serious refreshment; would you like an omelette?"

......

Feeling refreshed, the young couple continued their stroll up the gentle incline of Dorfstrasse. Passing a small park with a mini-golf course, Jo spotted that the entrance kiosk sold ice creams. "Do you fancy an ice cream?"

Two minutes later, they were sitting at a small table enjoying the ices and watching the antics of a family with two young children playing mini-golf. Whoops of merriment floated across the grass and even attracted the amused attention of passersby on the nearby road.

Jo looked delightedly at the children and turned towards David in a clear invitation to share the children's pleasure. "These last two days have been some of the happiest of my life!" she whispered.

"Mine too," he replied softly, squeezing the hand that lay beside him.

Jo felt so overjoyed that all she could do was to reciprocate his smile and make herself busy gathering up her rucksack ready for the return journey. They had already decided to run, or at least jog, up to Kleine Scheidegg again and then relax on the train and enjoy the scenic journey down to Lauterbrunnen.

......

The young couple set out in high spirits, jogging side by side where space allowed. By now they had become accustomed to each other's preferred pace and ran accordingly.

There were several changes of direction in the outskirts of the village, but, as they had found when coming in the opposite direction, the small yellow route markers bearing the black silhouette of a backpacker were invaluable. The gentle afternoon sunshine, combined with the mountain air, made jogging a pleasure, although they paused fairly frequently to admire the view and take a few sips of water.

"At least there are some places where the gradient eases up," David commented at one point.

Jo chuckled. "By the time we reach the top we'll have really achieved something today. Did I mention that my hope is for us to build up for a really challenging run that goes up through Mürren to the top of the Sefinenfurgge Pass, well over 500m higher than Kleine Scheidegg?"

"No, you didn't! But I'm game if you are!" David retorted, doing his best to sound as enthusiastic as his amazingly fit companion; the long slope they had just jogged steadily up had made considerable inroads into his energy reserves. At least Kleine Scheidegg was now in sight.

......

They just had time to get a quick take-away coffee before gratefully settling down in a train that was waiting to depart towards Wengen. Even Jo had to admit that it was nice to relax for the first time since leaving Grindelwald and the scenic journey became a delight as the train passed the Jungfrau, completely clear of cloud for the first time that day.

"It looks almost as amazing as it did yesterday morning," Jo said, her nose glued to the carriage window.

"Nothing could be quite like yesterday morning when we suddenly emerged from the trees!" David said. Jo looked at him and immediately knew what he meant.

Not long after leaving Wengernalp, the train crossed a meadow and Wengen came into sight nestling under a low mountain that formed the northern end of the ridge running all the way from Kleine Scheidegg.

"That's the Männlichen," Jo said when she saw David looking at it. "It's higher than Kleine Scheidegg and I was going to suggest climbing up there tomorrow if it's not too cloudy. There're said to be lovely views in all directions from the top."

"And we could see a little more of Wengen itself," David replied.

After that, it did not seem long before the train drew slowly into the village in question and the carriage filled up rapidly with tourists returning to their hotels and guesthouses in the valley and further afield. After waiting a short time to allow an upward-bound train pass, they moved off again on the steep descent.

"What a wonderful day!" Jo exclaimed as they entered the hotel and collected their keys from the reception desk. Climbing the stairs, she added. "See you at 6:30pm?"

David nodded and kissed her cheek before continuing up the stairs; he was on the floor above.

......

The evening meal was another pleasant occasion for both of them. Afterwards Jo declined the offer of a hot drink in the café visited the previous evening and opted instead for a stroll down to the river.

"I love the sound of rushing water and it'll be lovely down there in the gathering dusk," she said. "After that, another early night; it's a climb of over 1500m to the top of the Männlichen!"

David walked beside her with his arm around her waist. There was something very special about being with her and he had never felt so relaxed. This still came as rather a surprise; usually, when taking a potential girlfriend on a date, his sense of excitement was marred by the fear that he would put a foot wrong. In contrast, and quite amazingly, Jo seemed to accept him just as he was – faults and all.

The sound of water added an extra sense of peace to the tranquil night air and the strolling couple barely noticed the occasional car passing on the nearby road; they were in their own private world. At one point when nobody was in sight, they came together in a warm embrace. If there had been any remaining doubt about God's involvement in their meeting it was totally dispelled during that short but very special time beside the Lütschine.

CHAPTER 4: The Männlichen

Jo and David were having a quick water stop on a bench near Wengen station not long after ten o'clock. Then, after a brief visit to the nearby Coop to purchase a few provisions, they walked north up the main thoroughfare – another Dorfstrasse – pausing occasionally to look at the window displays.

Overlooking the far end of the street was a hotel with a spacious terrace that stood well above the level of the road. Several people were enjoying drinks at tables set out amongst small trees and potted plants.

"What a pleasant place to sit!" Jo murmured and David made a mental note

They left the centre of the village, aided by the yellow Männlichen signs positioned at almost every turn, and it was not long before they entered a steep wooded slope leading up to the crest of the ridge below which they had run to Kleine Scheidegg on their first morning.

Here Jo took the lead again and so began a long tough jog of twice the distance and height of the one up to Wengen. "What a girl!" David thought fondly as he followed on the heels of his athletic companion.

At first, the conifer trees were so dense that it was extremely gloomy, only alleviated by occasional shafts of light that managed to penetrate tiny gaps in the thick canopy. Eventually, however, the trees thinned and allowed glimpses back towards the valley. The gradient was now so severe that even Jo was reduced to a scramble, much to David's relief.

"She's fitter than I am!" he muttered to himself. It could be that Jo picked up his faint words because he thought he detected a chuckle above the measured sound of her breathing.

At one point, the sharp tip of a mountain bearing a small cap of snow came briefly into view. "Is that the Männlichen?" David called breathlessly.

"No, I think it must be the Tschuggen," Jo panted as she stopped and reached for her water bottle. "It's on this ridge but nearer Kleine Scheidegg and about 200m higher than the peak we're heading for."

Eventually, they were completely out in the open and jogging on narrow well-constructed path that climbed obliquely across a meadow of coarse grass. Such was the steepness of the slope plunging down towards Wengen that long sections of stout metal avalanche barriers were positioned at strategic intervals.

The clouds had now dispersed sufficiently to open up a splendid view of the valley floor and, even better, the tall mountains in the far south. The familiar peak of the Jungfrau was also visible beyond the end of the ridge.

Now began a superb zigzag climb to the top of the ridge at a point not far below the Männlichen summit. "This is incredible!" David called and Jo waved in reply.

"It certainly is!" agreed a loud voice in English not far above them. The surprised couple looked up; two men were descending the next higher leg of the zigzag. The four of them met at the corner and stopped briefly to exchange friendly greetings.

"We've come up from Grindelwald and are going down to Lauterbrunnen," one of them volunteered.

"We'll then take the train back," his friend added. "Are you doing the same in reverse? We can thoroughly recommend the path on the other side; the views are fantastic!"

"We may well do that," David said, "but haven't decided yet."

"Have a good time anyway," was the cheerful reply as the two men moved on.

"Let's decide when we reach the summit," Jo suggested as she started off again.

......

With mounting excitement, the young couple emerged on a broad gravel path running along the top of the ridge. A short distance below them was a small white building, clearly the terminus of the cable car coming up from Wengen. Beyond lay the splendid panorama of the Tschuggen backed by the Eiger, Mönch and Jungfrau in almost all their glory: almost because there were still a few small clouds clinging stubbornly to the peaks.

A cable car had obviously just arrived because a large group of people had emerged from the building and were coming in the direction of the Männlichen.

"We'd better get moving," David said. "I'd dearly like to be with you alone on the summit!"

"I doubt if we'll be that lucky," Jo said as they moved off at a brisk jog.

But his wish was granted. Although they jogged past several hikers, the observation platform on the summit itself was deserted. In delight, he grabbed hold of his beloved and swung her round in a dancer's twirl while she laughed for sheer joy. Then they sobered up and gradually rotated clockwise in take in the breathtaking view.

To the northwest, Interlaken lay deep in the mist and out of sight at the entrance to the Y-shaped valley. Then their gaze swept along the formidable arc of the north-eastern flank of the Grindelwald valley, followed by the Wetterhorn standing serenely behind the village itself. To the southeast came the grand sweep of the famous three, commencing with the stern grey bulk of the Eiger guarding the way to the more appealing Mönch and Jungfrau. Finally, after taking in the mountainous backdrop of the Lauterbrunnen valley itself, they peered over the safety balustrade at Wengen nestling far below them.

This last sight gave David an idea. "Why don't we run along the top of this ridge past the Tschuggen to Kleine Scheidegg, have some late refreshments there and then run back to Wengen for coffee or tea before taking the train for the rest of the way to Lauterbrunnen?"

"We'll certainly need to refill our water bottles and have a long cold drink at Kleine Scheidegg, but don't forget that we're already carrying a few things for lunch!" Jo reminded him.

"So we are! My rucksack feels so light that I'd forgotten; I must be getting tougher already!" David retorted. "We could have a picnic looking down at Grindelwald from the slopes of the Tschuggen."

They moved off just as the large party of tourists from the cable car arrived at the summit.

......

It turned out to be a splendid run to Kleine Scheidegg, for most part on a descending path.

"This is a welcome change after so much climbing!" David shouted cheerfully, feeling on top of the world almost literally, such was the beauty of their surroundings and his delight at being with Jo. This was amplified even further by the fact that the width of the track allowed them to run side by side.

They soon passed the Wengen cable station and, only a short distance further, a hotel beside another cable station that, from the direction of its cables, clearly descended into Grindelwald.

The path narrowed considerably and wound its way over a long wide meadow sprinkled with alpine plants, before eventually dropping down from the crest to cling to the eastern flank of the Tschuggen. Here they found a convenient rock overlooking Grindelwald valley for their picnic lunch.

"I think we've come about halfway; Kleine Scheidegg should be less than two miles now," Jo said.

Ten minutes later, they moved on. There followed what was probably the most spectacular part of the run as the narrow path snaked its way along the flank of the rocky mountain, descending gradually most of the time. The scenery was dominated by the Eiger, but quite often the many twists in the path pointed them directly towards the Wetterhorn, now thinly veiled in haze.

A large building eventually appeared not far ahead, followed moments later by the sight of Kleine Scheidegg a short distance below. "I think that must be the Restaurant Grindelwaldblick," Jo volunteered. "Somebody mention it yesterday. What about having a convenience stop and drink here?"

"That's a good idea," David agreed. "Its terrace probably has an even better view than the one at the station."

The terrace was indeed a pleasant place to sit. It also gave David the opportunity to observe Jo's delightful profile as she enjoyed a cold refreshing drink and gazed out at the surrounding scenery. Although this was now their third day together, his deep thankfulness for their first unexpected encounter was still growing. Everything about her appealed to him: her delightful heart-shaped face and hazel-green eyes, her near perfect athletic body, her astonishing fitness and stamina, and, above all, her gentle nature that seemed to reach out and draw him to her. In short, Jo was sheer joy to be with and he wanted to be with her forever!

They were having such a special time together that it was quite a shock when Jo looked at her watch and exclaimed: "If we want to see a bit more of Wengen before getting the train to Lauterbrunnen, we'd better get moving!"

They gathered their things and left, not even pausing in Kleine Scheidegg. In fact, they made such good time on the downhill run that they were back at Wengen station soon after four o'clock. Entering Dorfstrasse, they almost immediately passed a nice looking patisserie, prompting David to ask: "Would you like coffee and cake?"

Not surprisingly, the idea appealed to his companion. They were not disappointed: the selection was even better than in Lauterbrunnen and, within minutes, they were sharing a tasty slice of cake and discussing plans for tomorrow.

Jo had an immediate suggestion. "Assuming the weather permits, are you ready for our hardest trail run yet, going up through Mürren and Spielbodenalp to the top of the Sefinenfurgge Pass at just over 2600m? There and back is about 22 miles but involves a climb of 1800m!"

David looked at her and smiled at her obvious enthusiasm; he was prepared to go anywhere with such a companion. "Of course I am," he replied, matching her eagerness.

They left the pleasant patisserie and its enticing aroma of coffee, sugar and spices to explore some of the quaint narrow streets of the village, before happily returning to the station for the train back to Lauterbrunnen.

Chapter 5: Interlaken

David woke to the sound of rain drumming on the broad metal gutter just above the window. Pulling back the curtains he could see thick cloud obscuring the top of the cliff and even the nearby Staubbach Falls were almost out of sight.

"Not much chance of a long run today!" he thought sadly as he descended the stairs to Jo's bedroom on the floor below. They exchanged a good-morning hug prior to going down for breakfast and looking out of the large picture window at the dismal scene.

"I think the only solution for today is a trip to Interlaken; it's said to be a nice place. Anyway, I need to find a couple of small holiday gifts for my parents and younger brother and the choice will be better there," Jo said. "Are you happy to come?"

"You bet! And you've reminded me that I must get something for my parents," David replied, willing to do any amount of sightseeing and window shopping if he could be with his beloved.

The same happy smile returned to his face almost an hour later when he sat opposite Jo on the train. She seemed full of beans and was clearly looking forward to the day ahead, although it looked likely to be quite a wet one. They were clad in hooded anoraks and had light waterproof over-trousers in their backpacks as a precaution against even heavier rain.

......

It was only when descending the steps to the pedestrian tunnel under the railway tracks at Interlaken Ost that it occurred to David to suggest leaving the station on the northern side so that they could have a quick look at the River Aare.

"I remember glimpsing the river several times when I first arrived," he said. "It runs through the town connecting Lake Thun to Lake Brienz and the train coming in from Berne crosses it several times after leaving Interlaken West at the end of Lake Thun."

"Yes, and I think we'll find the terminus for the Lake Brienz steamers here!" Jo added.

She turned out to be correct and they found themselves immediately opposite a small park, across which a paved path led directly to the riverside quay. There was even a steamer waiting to depart, all but the hardiest passengers sheltering from the rain in the large saloon. A Swiss flag flapped proudly, if rather damply, from its stern post.

The vessel moved off, its large paddles churning the water as they struggled against the strong current. Eventually the battle was won and the last the young couple saw was the wave of the red and white flag as the steamer rounded a curve in the river.

Leaving the quay, Jo opened a small umbrella and she and David squeezed together under its meagre protection, although, very thankfully, the rain was now much lighter. Turning right, they passed the venerable Hotel Du Lac and crossed the tracks towards the centre of the town.

The narrow riverside park continued beyond the hotel until they came to what was obviously one of the major routes through the town – the Höheweg – judging by its width and the increasingly posh hotels. They were soon standing outside a large one proudly announcing itself to be the Lindner Grand Hotel Beau Rivage.

"I bet a night there costs as much as a week's half-board where we are," David surmised.

"And that probably doesn't include breakfast!" Jo added. "I remember watching a TV programme about one of the smart London hotels; rooms there started at about £1000 and the top suite was astronomical!"

"But probably include a personal butler!" he quipped back. But Jo was now more interested in gazing through the windows of a wood-carving shop and David took her hand while they admired some of the remarkable feats of craftsmanship.

A little further on, more palatial hotels appeared and had the benefit of overlooking a park on the south side of the road. Far beyond, the lower slopes of several mountains could just be discerned through the mist and drizzle.

After passing several expensive looking shops and cafés, they came to the largest hotel they had ever seen. It consisted of two enormous wings linked together by an impressive lobby with "Victoria Jungfrau" emblazed in gold letters above its entrance.

"That must be yet another 5-star hotel; I wonder how many there are in this town," Jo remarked as they moved on.

Soon the park ended and the road narrowed to make way for shops on both sides. Then, to Jo's delight, she saw a quaint pedestrian precinct leading off to the left. Even the drizzle had almost stopped and she folded her umbrella before taking David's hand to walk slowly down it, pausing from time to time as she spotted one interesting thing after another. By the time, they had reached the end of the short passage and entered a pleasant little square, she had a present for her parents safely packed in her rucksack.

"Now comes the harder job of finding something for Brian; he's sixteen and very difficult to please!" she explained.

"You could always fall back on chocolates; I expect that's what I'll get for my parents," David said. "But now, what about a cup of coffee?" he added hopefully.

It took a surprisingly long time to find a café that was not too crowded. "The rain has driven more people into the town than usual," Jo said as they thankfully took off their anoraks to sit at a table in a café tucked up an insignificant little side street. It turned out to be a pleasant place to sip coffee in comfort, looking out at the rain that had started again.

"We've been down so many streets that I've completely lost my bearings," David admitted. "When I pay the bill, I'll ask the waitress for directions to the West station. It should be easy to find our way back to Interlaken Ost from there."

......

As it happened, the young couple found themselves passing a huge Migros supermarket when they followed the directions given.

"Let's explore in here," David said. "It's past one o'clock and there'll almost certainly be a café serving snacks at reasonable cost."

"And we may solve the rest of our gift problem!" Jo added with a feeling of relief.

The place was enormous with several departments, and, as David had guessed, one of them was a very good self-service café where they treated themselves to a light meal.

"This is surprisingly good," Jo remarked appreciatively as they sat at one end of a table for six, most of the smaller tables still being in use even at such a late hour. "You'd be hard pressed to find this quality in a British supermarket café."

Afterwards they wandered around in the vain hope of finding some suitable and reasonable gifts, but, in the end, were forced to fall back on a couple of boxes of Swiss chocolates.

"It's the thought that counts," Jo said sadly. "The sort of thing that might have pleased Brian would have been ridiculously expensive: quite outside my budget."

"Not to mention heavy to carry home," David added.

Chapter 6: A Day to Remember

The following day the sky was almost clear with very few clouds still clinging to the higher ground and sunshine was streaming through the picture window of the hotel restaurant when Jo and David came down to an early breakfast.

"Are you ready for our challenge?" Jo said, looking at David hopefully.

He gave her a beaming smile. "I'm looking forward to it," he responded readily. What could be better than a run in glorious surroundings with the most wonderful girl in the world?

Jo was pleased. Not only was she looking forward to an adventure with the man she loved but it would have been risky to do anything so ambitious on her own. Although the outward journey was only about eleven miles, they would be climbing considerably higher than Kleine Scheidegg on what might turn out to be a difficult path.

......

Soon after eight o'clock the young couple were already climbing a path zigzagging up the western side of the valley towards Winteregg, a station on the cliff-top railway halfway between Mürren and the cable station above Lauterbrunnen. At first, the path was extremely steep and frequently stepped but eventually they were able to jog more easily and it was not long before a large restaurant appeared and then Winteregg station itself. The path then joined a wide cliff-top track that followed the railway the rest of the way to Mürren.

The views became even better as Jo followed the yellow Sefinenfurgge route signs southwest out of the village. She called for a water stop when they reached a point where the direction signs offered a choice of route: either the narrow road they had been following or a path.

"The website I consulted says this road is the easiest way to Spielbodenalp, where you'll be pleased to learn there's a small restaurant. However, it recommends the path as an even more scenic alternative," she said.

"Let's take the path then," David replied, "as long as we don't miss the coffee!"

They set off again in happy anticipation of what was to come and were not disappointed. The path skirted dense thickets of conifers and wound its way over delightful little meadows. The glorious view to their left, beyond the southern end of the main valley, was dominated by the snow-capped Grosshorn and Breithorn.

Soon the path left the trees behind altogether and gradually turned in a more westerly direction. "There's the 3000m Schilthorn!" Jo exclaimed, pointing directly ahead. "You know; the mountain with the famous revolving restaurant at the top."

"Mainly famous because most of the action in one of the James Bond 007 films takes place there," David added, taking the opportunity to have a quick drink.

The view to the north was dominated by the formidable Birg, a grey ridge on which there was a transfer point for the Schilthorn cable cars coming up from Mürren. "Not so nice," was Jo's muttered comment as she stowed her own water bottle.

They moved on and soon bore left away from the Schilthorn, eventually crossing a stream before arriving on a broad meadow basking under the midmorning sun. It was dotted with small farm buildings and a gust of breeze carried the gentle clang of cowbells from somewhere out of sight. It was an oasis of tranquillity.

"This whole area is Spielbodenalp; I think we have to go a little further to find your long-awaited coffee," Jo said with a smile.

David grinned back at her. "Don't pretend you don't want one too!"

It was not long before they reached the small building and sat outside enjoying the sunshine not far from a family with two teenage children. From the conversation, it was clear that the small group had hiked up from the cable station in Mürren and were just about to return the same way. Especially exciting for the youngsters had been the ride up in the cable car and they were eagerly anticipating the downward passage to the car park in the Lauterbrunnen valley.

"I passed that car park and cable station on the way to Stechelberg to join a path up to Mürren on my first morning here," Jo whispered.

Twenty minutes later, the young couple left Spielbodenalp and its delightful surroundings. This marked the start of by far the best part of that incredible day running and jogging through stunning sun-bathed scenery and invigorating mountain air. The easy gradient of the last two miles or so was behind them and the path soon began to climb as it traversed the flank of a grassy slope dotted with conifers. In fact, it zigzagged and undulated so much that it was quite hard to negotiate at reasonable speed.

It gradually became clear that their route was heading towards a bend in the ridge and would soon run in an even more westerly direction high above a narrow offshoot of the main valley. The view behind them was still dominated by the Jungfrau massif and would continue to be so all the way to Sefinenfurgge, but now, as the path climbed, more and more of what had previously been hidden emerged.

After climbing about 200m, Jo and David stopped for drink and turned to look back. To the southeast, they were confronted by an unbroken chain of snow-covered mountains stretching out towards the west.

"How wonderful," Jo whispered.

David nodded. "None of those mountains is as high as the Jungfrau but I had no idea there were so many. Being lower down certainly limits the view! One of them must be the

Breithorn although I can't pick it out from here because our viewing angle has changed."

"Look a little further north!" his companion exclaimed, pointing again. "I'm sure I can see the top of the Wetterhorn!"

Sure enough, their higher altitude and new angle of view now meant that the beautiful mountain had appeared beyond the Eiger.

But the splendid mountain panorama was only part of that wonderful scene. Not only could Mürren be seen in the distance, but also, now far below them, the expanse of conifer-fringed meadows and tiny ribbon-like path they had traversed not long before. Nearer at hand, this path had just crested the brow of the slope and so they now stood on almost level ground but with the ridge continuing to rise to their left: so steeply that several areas of sheer rock towered above them.

Almost reluctantly, David, who had been leading for the last half hour, set off again, with Jo close behind, but she determined to remember this delightful spot and spend time there on the way back.

The pleasant path continued to thread its way across an alpine meadow, fragrant with wild flowers, before dropping sharply to reveal another splendid spectacle. At the bottom of a hanging valley were two buildings – tiny at this distance – sitting below a 2800m ridge composed of massive rocky crags partly concealed by small wispy clouds that were slowly coalescing and fragmenting in the wind. Expanses of grey shale, dotted with patches of snow, warned of a difficult climb ahead after negotiating the lower grass-covered slopes.

Jo stopped to survey the scene. "The buildings down there must be the Rotstockhütte – a restaurant with a lodge for hikers – and I think the Sefinenfurgge Pass is tucked behind that huge buttress of rock jutting out from the ridge."

Just then a brief gust of wind parted the mist and revealed a U-shaped notch in the formidable barrier. "There it is," she cried. "Let's get going."

There was a hint of relish in her words and David smiled. "That's my girl!" he thought fondly.

Led by Jo, they descended eagerly and passed close to the modest buildings before jogging over the undulating slopes leading up to the band of shale. Their final challenge had commenced; a climb of over 500m.

The gradient steepened as the path snaked upward but Jo was determined to keep jogging, however slowly, and was only reduced to a careful scramble when the shale became even steeper and more unstable. Eventually, just under an hour after leaving Rotstockhütte she crested the gap and peered down the other side, breathing heavily but full of elation.

A couple of seconds later David joined her and gathered her in a bear hug. "You're incredible! ... Super fit... and the... most marvellous... girl in the world!" he managed to gasp between huge intakes of breath.

His words thrilled Jo to the core, but, to cover her embarrassment, she drew his attention to the rather bleak downward slope of dull grey shale and snow on the far side. It was even steeper than the slope they had just climbed. Some wooden steps had been set into the steepest section, up which three weary hikers were slowly climbing in single file.

"I'm rather glad we're turning back at this point," she joked. "Now we'd better take in the view back towards Mürren before this place gets crowded!"

She took David's hand and they scrambled down a short distance to get clear of an enormous chunk of rock that was getting in the way. Their favourite mountains once again dominated the magnificent view; the Jungfrau, Mönch, Eiger and Wetterhorn stretched out towards the northeast.

"More of the Wetterhorn is visible from this height. It's all so beautiful!" David said appreciatively.

"It certainly is," Jo agreed, "but, even so, we've not found anything to surpass our first sighting of the northern face of the Jungfrau at close quarters!"

"And I think I know why," came the quiet reply.
......

Jo and David descended the unstable shale with care and only speeded up when reaching the narrow path winding and dipping its way over the grassy slope. After a brief refreshment stop at Rotstockhütte, they moved on without a pause until reaching the viewpoint that had so impressed Jo on the way up. Here she suggested a water stop and a chance to revel in the splendid view. She extracted a bottle of water and anorak from her rucksack and laid the latter out for them to sit on.

"It'll also give me a chance to hear how you became a Christian; all you've told me so far is that it happened very suddenly in your second year at university, so fire away," she said, patting the space beside her.

"I was confined to bed for a couple of days with 'flu," David began slowly. "A friend popped in for a brief visit and left a book on my bedside table with the casual comment: "If you haven't anything else to read, this might help!"

"A little later and wanting something to take my mind off my aches and pains, I picked it up and saw that it had an intriguing title, "The Message". Opening it in the middle, my eyes were greeted by "Isaiah 53" at the top of a page – it was only a Bible after all! About to snap it shut in disappointment, my eyes caught a short passage:

"We're all like sheep who have wandered off and got lost. We've all done our own thing, gone our own way. And God has pilled all our sins, everything we've done wrong, on him, on him."

"I had a sufficient religious background to know that the "him" was Jesus Christ and I was certainly feeling very lost at the time; not only extremely grotty with the 'flu but wondering if the subject I had chosen to study was the right one or even if I should have been at university at all! To be honest, I was also getting increasingly uncomfortable about the way I was living my life; everything seemed to lack purpose.

"As I pondered on Isaiah's poignant words in such simple English, my thumb slipped and a large chunk of pages flipped over and I found myself looking at the heading "Ephesians". I gazed in bewilderment, never having come across the name before. Then a short sentence almost literally stood out from the page. "It's in Christ that we live to find out who we are and what we are living for," it declared.

"I can't describe the impact these words had on me. It was as if the meaning of everything was contained in them; that the focal point of the universe was one single person: Jesus Christ. And somehow I knew that this certainty was not a product of my own imagination or thought processes but had come from outside myself.

I felt tears running down my cheeks. The God I had never believed in was calling me and I was being invited to respond. But how? I had never prayed before. Then I suddenly remembered my grandmother. I had stayed with her as a child – sometimes for days at a time – and every evening she would lead me in the old traditional form of the Lord's Prayer before I got into bed; so many times that I still knew it by heart. Would that do? Hopefully I began:

"Our Father, who art in heaven, hallowed be thy name; thy kingdom come; thy will be done...." The familiar words were strangely comforting, but it was only when I came to the words: "And forgive us our trespasses," that I felt impelled to pause and add the rest of the sentence with just as much meaning and emphasis, "as we forgive those who trespass against us," that something extraordinary happened. It was as if a current of electricity ran through my body burning something up as it passed. For a fleeting second, I felt completely empty but then incredible joy filled me and I knew without a shadow of doubt that I had been completely forgiven; all my sins, known and unknown, had been wiped out.

"It was only later when I thanked my friend and explained what had occurred that he helped me understand more clearly the meaning of Jesus dying a totally undeserved death on the Cross so that the sins of everyone prepared to believe can be forgiven and completely forgotten by God.

"So this is my rather strange story; I've told it to very few people because it does seem unusual, to say the least, but I only know that I have never looked back or had any doubts."

David lapsed into silence, wondering what Jo might think, but she took his hand and squeezed it. "Thank you for sharing something so personal!" she whispered, giving him one of her wonderful smiles.

He looked at her, now slightly anxious, but the time was ripe. "How could I do otherwise," he said slowly, "when I have completely fallen in love with you and want to ask you to marry me?"

Jo gave a little gasp and threw her arms around his neck. "I will, ... I will!" she cried. They kissed as they had never kissed before and then sat in a happy daze looking out over the glorious scene.

It was several minutes before they ran on in a state of complete euphoria and almost without a pause until reaching Mürren. Here they had a quick glass of tea on a sunny terrace before descending to Lauterbrunnen just in time for a quick shower before dinner.

There was plenty to discuss over the meal, not least when they should each meet their respective parents-in-law and start making preparations for the wedding ceremony.

"I'm determined to keep everything as simple as possible," Jo declared at one point, "not least because my parents are not very well off."

"I expect mine will chip in, but I'm also for simplicity," David assured her. "You will look stunning in the simplest of dresses!"

The last few words had been whispered because he was suddenly conscious that the small dining room was quite full by now. It was only when they were out for their evening stroll that he continued what he had wanted to say: "Have I told you that you're the most beautiful girl in the world and I adore you?"

Jo was too moved to reply but flung her arms around his neck and kissed him, eventually managing to whisper: "I love you more than I can possibly say!"

A short time later, on their way back to the hotel, she said: "Getting engaged this afternoon was the icing on the cake, but I've also enjoyed every minute of our run today. What about attempting something even tougher next week after taking it easier for a day or two?"

"By all means," David responded eagerly, feeling he was game for anything, especially now that it would be with his new fiancée no less! "What do you have in mind?"

"To go up the Sefinenfurgge again and continue on over the Hohtürli Pass to Kandersteg, a total distance of nearly 24 miles if we take a shortcut between the two passes. It should be possible to do it in just over eight hours. There's a good train service back here via Spiez and Interlaken; the cost shouldn't be too bad with our half-price travel cards."

"It sounds a superb challenge; if we can do that successfully we'll have really achieved something," David replied, hugging her. "I must have one of the fittest and toughest fiancée's in the whole world!"

A few minutes later, as they were about part outside her bedroom, Jo chuckled. "I failed to tell you that the Hohtürli is 150m higher than the Sefinenfurgge!" she whispered. Then, when she saw a trace of concern on David's face, she added: "But the shortcut I mentioned avoids going all the way down into the hamlet of Griesalp and so the Hohtürli climb starts at about 1600m: twice the height of Lauterbrunnen."

Chapter 7: A Real Challenge

Thus it was that three days later, after a couple of active but easier days, Jo and David set out well before eight o'clock on their toughest challenge so far. The weather was slightly overcast, but the clouds were above the lower mountain tops and so they decided to risk it. Their brief water stops were shorter than before and they made much better time to the top of the Sefinenfurgge, their only coffee break having been at Rotstockhütte.

"You're amazing!" David declared breathlessly as he and Jo rested in the narrow gap looking back towards the Jungfrau and its companions, still topped with cloud. As he recovered, he realized with pleasure that, although faster, the climb had not taken as much out of him as previously; he had obviously become fitter and more acclimatized to high altitude running.

......

On the western side of the Pass, the two runners were confronted with large areas of barren grey rock, shale and patches of thick snow. As they carefully descended the wooden steps first seen three days earlier, the view north revealed an ugly craggy mountain that was clearly part of the ridge they had just crested. To the south lay a much higher broad-shouldered mountain – as evidenced by the amount of snow on top. It was almost completely clear of cloud and there were even hints in that direction that the sun might put in an appearance before too long.

"What a splendid mountain!" David exclaimed as he followed Jo downwards.

"That's the Blüemlisalphorn massive," she called back. "The main peak is well short of 4000m but it dominates the Kandersteg valley."

"A mere tiddler then ...." David started to chuckle but then began coughing; he had just shared a rather crumbly fruit and nut bar with Jo during their recent water stop.

Jo stopped to thumb him on the back. "We'd better stop talking and concentrate on the task in hand," she advised.

The path soon left the shale behind and descended over coarse grass strewn with small rocks. At one point the route took them down a narrow gorge beside a fast-flowing stream where it was necessary to proceed with care; it would certainly not do to twist an ankle at this stage of the journey.

The narrow valley widened and it became clear that they had been following a cleft in the side of the ridge; a seemingly vast valley lay before them backed by yet another long range of low peaks. Jo stopped and suggested that David take the lead again down a path that wound its way over a slope of coarse grass liberally scattered with rocky outcrops.

"We'll soon pass a refreshment hut for weary hikers, although we don't have time to stop," she explained. "Not long after that there should be a sign on the left-hand side pointing towards Bundalp. So keep an eye out; we don't want to go all the way down into Griesalp!"

They ran on, thankful that the path was a good one, and it was not long before they reached the Bundalp turning. Here, the climbing began again and David led them at a steady jog up the undulating slope, conserving energy for what was to come.

......

Bundalp turned out to have a sizeable alpine lodge with restaurant set in a high alpine pasture overlooking a narrow road that had come up from Griesalp over 400m below. It was pleasant to relax for a short time on the terrace with mugs of hot chocolate ("We probably need the sugar," Jo had advised) and gazing out at the surrounding grass and rock covered ridges and the higher mountains beyond.

Then, almost reluctant to leave such a pleasant place, they moved on with Jo now leading. It was tough going, although the real challenge had not yet begun, but the runners were cheered by the beautiful scenery and gentle afternoon sun.

Most of the clouds had dispersed revealing a magnificent view of the mountain range to the southeast of the Hohtürli Pass.

Leaving the grass slopes behind, the path began traversing the ugly grey scree in zigzags that clung desperately to the steep slope. Jo jogged on determinedly and David, only a few feet behind, caught a sense of her pleasure at this test of endurance on a really serious and sustained gradient. Such was his affinity with her that he found himself similarly endowed with the determination not to falter.

During a brief pause for water, the young couple looked back at the panorama they were leaving behind. The route recently negotiated had shrunk to a thin writhing ribbon far below them, and, over to the east, the Sefinenfurgge Pass was merely a tiny notch in the saddle between two mountains. Further north, a misty patch of water had come into view at the end of a distant valley.

"That must be Lake Thun!" Jo exclaimed. "It shows how high we are."

Two sets of legs were definitely feeling the effect of climbing almost 900m after the descent from the previous vantage point. In the forward direction, however, it was a great encouragement to see the Hohtürli Pass not far above them.

The path became even steeper and Jo was reduced to a steady climb or even scramble in places where the scree was slippery. Eventually they reached the bottom of a long flight of wooden steps curving round a base of a cliff into which had been set a cable handrail. Quite thick snow lay to their left and even reached the step in places.

Near the top, they spotted a wooden bench and sat for a few moments sipping more water and gazing back towards the Sefinenfurgge ridge for the last time. It was quite a shock to realize that they were now at an even higher elevation. Then Jo pointed to a grey-stone building on the ridge just above them, a Swiss flag flapping proudly from a nearby flag pole. "That's Blümlisalphütte where we can get a drink," she said.

"Good," David responded gratefully.

A final short climb took them up to the welcome sight. Although well over 100 years old, it turned out to be the best café-cum-alpine lodge they had been in so far and the Hohtürli Pass was not much more than 200 yards away.

"Only the Swiss could be so well organised," Jo commented as they sat on the steep terrace enjoying a short rest and a drink; even a glass of tea was welcome after all their exertion.

"Well, they've been in the tourist industry for a long time and certainly have the right landscape for it. Just look at these views!" David exclaimed.

......

The initial descent from the Hohtürli involved several flights of steps as the narrow path took them in a series of switchbacks across an extensive area of shale scree and barren grey rock. It was quite hard on the thighs, but at least they were encouraged by a glimpse of Kandersteg in the far distance, backed by yet another formidable ridge.

Pausing for a few sips of water a short time later, Jo pointed: "Look up there to our left. Those stretches of ice and snow between those buttresses of rock are glaciers flowing down from the Blüemlisalphorn. Aren't they splendid?"

David nodded in acknowledgement but he was more interested in the route they were following. It appeared to be descending into an eastern side-branch of the very long valley that ran all the way north from Kandersteg to Spiez on Lake Thun. Although their near surroundings could best be described as stark and wild, there was the promise of far better to come.

On top of it all, he had the joy of accompanying the girl he loved more than he had ever thought possible. Not only did they both delight in trail running and excelled at it – although she even more than he – but they were discovering that they were kindred spirits in so many other ways.

The path continued to lose height as it skirted overhanging rocks and clung precariously to the steep side of a long ridge, but, at last, the coarse grass returned and the young couple found themselves crossing peaceful pastures above Ober Bergli where they were surprised to see yet another hut providing refreshments.

"We don't have time to stop for more than a short water break and to admire the scenery," Jo said.

But what scenery! A tranquil lake of bluish water nestled not far below them, sheltering within an arc formed by the Blüemlisalphorn and two other snow-capped mountains, their flanks sloping directly down into the water.

"That's Oeschinensee – the famous Blue Lake – about 600m above Kandersteg," Jo said. "It's a popular tourist spot for people visiting the area. Before I came away, I found out that the railway line from Spiez enters a long tunnel just south of Kandersteg and ends up in Brig."

"Yes, I read about that; it's the Lötschberg tunnel completed in 1907," David replied. "Brig is also at the northern end of the Simplon tunnel linking Switzerland to Italy."

The young couple continued to follow the narrow path as it continued west obliquely down the steep flank of the slope bounding the northern side of the lake. Eventually, they reached the shore itself where a smooth flat path skirted the water's edge and led to the Berghaus – a hotel/restaurant at the western end of the lake. The tables on the terrace overlooking the beautiful blue-tinged water and surrounding mountains were still very busy although it was nearly three-thirty. Here they stopped for water and a short rest before the final leg of the journey.

"There's a cable lift not far away but we mustn't cheat! There's only just over two miles to go now and it's all downhill," Jo said cheerfully.

David looked at her as he sipped from his flask, amazed that she still seemed to be relatively unfazed by the effort of their arduous run.

A few minutes later, they set off again with David leading. A signpost directed them along a road that soon descended steeply for nearly a mile before a walking sign on the left led to a pleasant path that followed the south side of a wide rocky stream and eventually took them across the meadows bordering Kandersteg.

......

A relieved but triumphant young couple made their way to the railway station and discovered that they only just had time to buy tickets before the next hourly train to Spiez. Swiss trains always run on time and so, a few minutes later, they were finally relaxing on comfortable seats and watching the world go by.

"I'm sorry there wasn't time to get any take-away coffee but I'll try in Spiez," David said apologetically. "Anyway, we've really achieved something today; not so much in the distance covered – a fairly modest 23 miles or so, but in those two long climbs! If I hadn't been with you, I don't think I'd have made the second one!"

"Yes, you would; you're tougher than you think. You were an inspiration to me," Jo replied, gripping his hand tightly.

They remained happily holding hands for the remainder of the short journey to Spiez but found that there was still no time to get any coffee because the Interlaken train was due within five minutes. It turned out to be an intercity express coming through from Basle and, as it drew to a halt, they were surprised to find themselves standing beside a buffet car labelled "Restaurant Bistro".

"Look! We can get a cup of coffee after all. There should be time to drink it before we get to Interlaken Ost," David said as they boarded.

The train terminated at Interlaken Ost and so the attendant was reluctant to serve them until he found out that they only wanted coffee. To David's surprise, the latter was the same price as in an ordinary café, but he added a larger tip than usual as a small thank you.

The young couple grinned happily at each other across the narrow table as they sipped the coffee. It was a novel experience for both of them, enhanced by being able to look out over Lake Thun as the train wound its way along the narrow strip of land between the water and adjacent slope, the track almost touching the water on occasion.

David looked out of both sides of the carriage and deduced that they were on a single track. This was confirmed when the train came to a halt at a small station for a minute or so, not to take on passengers but to allow a train to pass in the opposite direction.

"This is delightful," Jo said, smiling at her companion.

"And the coffee is far better than on a British train," he grinned back at her.

......

Even with such short waits for trains, the young couple only arrived back at their hotel in time for a shower before dinner. "Gosh, I'm hungry!" David muttered as they entered the dining room rather later than usual.

"So am I! We've had very little protein since a very early breakfast," Jo returned.

Fortunately, the soup was a thick one and the main course a generous portion of chicken casserole. It was while eating the latter that David remarked sadly: "I've only got two more nights in Switzerland. Tomorrow is my last full day!"

Jo nodded sympathetically. "I've only got three more nights here, but we must be thankful that our dates coincided so closely. I'm going to miss you on my final day!"

"We must do something really special tomorrow – rain or shine!" David promised.

Chapter 8: Mountain of Joy

Jo gave David a cheerful smile across the breakfast table the following morning. "Do you know what I'd really like to do today?" she asked shyly.

"Do tell me," David replied, ready to agree to anything his beloved desired.

"Go up through Wengen and take a picnic lunch to have at Wengernalp overlooking our favourite mountain. I want that scene and what happened up there to be firmly imprinted on my mind forever!"

David reached out and gripped her hand. "That's a wonderful idea," he whispered.

......

Two hours later the young couple were in the Coop in Wengen collecting things for a picnic in a wire basket. Although they had jogged almost all the way, David was delighted to find that the steep slope had not taken as much out of him as on the first occasion.

"Switzerland must have done me good," he thought, but then realized it was his companion who was responsible for most of the improvement.

Running together where the width of the track allowed, they continued up the long climb towards Wengernalp. The weather was rather mixed but they were so happy together that they did not mind. At least the sun was putting in an occasional appearance from behind the multitude of small clouds.

At the pace they ran it did not take very long to reach the point where the path was about to emerge from the tree line near the end of the ridge.

Here Jo slowed to a standstill and turned to offer her hand to David. He clasped it eagerly and they walked together, savouring the moment when they would see the Jungrau in all its glory and recall the wonderful moment when they had first looked at each other in its majestic presence and realized that they had, quite amazingly, also met their partner for life.

......

A cloud veiled part of the soaring peak but it was still magnificent. David led Jo across the meadow to an isolated spot overlooking the glorious sight and they stood in a gentle embrace. Jo gave a happy little sigh and laid her head against his chest.

"I love you more than I can say," he whispered, but then realized mere words were inadequate and that the only response to the depth of love between them was inner silence. And so they stood completely still; the only sound the whoosh of the gentle breeze and the faint voices of passing hikers.

Even the latter faded away to total silence and the young couple found themselves enfolded in a presence far greater and more wonderful than the surrounding scenery. Filled with a mixture of awe and joy, they recognized the presence of their Lord and Saviour.

The experience only lasted a minute or so but it was more than enough to assure them of his blessing over their relationship, marriage and future together. With the eye of faith they also knew that Jesus would never leave them nor forsake them, however difficult the path of life might turn out to be.

The faint background noises returned and, with one accord, Jo and David turned and walked hand in hand to find a bench for their picnic lunch. They were unaware that, for a brief moment, radiance followed in their wake.

The End

NEVER RUN ALONE (Part Two)
Chapter 1: Jason

Jason walked slowly across University Square on the campus of Birmingham University in an attempt to unwind. He felt in need of a cup of strong coffee, but, having just emerged from his PhD oral examination, the adrenaline was still surging around his body and he thought it would be wise to let it dissipate before consuming another stimulant.

Although he was confident he had made substantial progress with the subject of his thesis – magnetic waves in the Sun's corona – the principal external examiner had been determined to press him hard. It was helpful that his supervisor had warned him of the man's reputation beforehand and had even broken normal convention by springing to Jason's defence once during the session itself.

"Professor X is one of those hard-liners who believe that higher-degree candidates should be forced to defend their dissertations, even if he is privately happy with the content," the friendly man had said the day prior to the oral.

Jason had been extremely relieved when, after a very long eighty minutes, his interrogator settled back in his chair and glanced at the second examiner – an eminent female physicist who had asked several astute but helpful questions – before smiling at Jason in an avuncular manner and uttering the words every PhD candidate longs to hear: "Off the record, I'm sure we will all be recommending to the University's Examination Board that your thesis be approved without alteration, apart from a few small typos. Well done!"

With those reassuring words ringing in his ears, Jason had thanked the assembled company and left the room.

......

Seated at a refectory table with his coffee, Jason contemplated what he should do after completing the relatively simple task of replacing a few pages in the loosely bound copies of the thesis, using the list of corrections his supervisor would no doubt give him tomorrow, and then taking the precious volumes to be properly bound.

He badly needed a holiday before commencing his first job in five weeks time with the Institute of Gravitational Research in Glasgow. Although Birmingham had a similar research group, it was time he moved on after spending nearly seven years of his life there, first as an undergraduate then postgraduate in the Department of Physics and Astronomy. His mother would miss him but Glasgow was not all that far away.

His birth parents had died tragically in a motorway accident when he was twelve years of age and Social Services had allowed his aunt and uncle to adopt him after a trial period of fostering. This had worked out very well, Jason already being accustomed to frequent contact with his close relatives, and it was not long before it became quite natural to call them Mum and Dad.

Very sadly, his adoptive father had died of cancer soon after Jason commenced his undergraduate studies. It was good that he had chosen to study in Birmingham and live at home because his mother had needed support during her time of grief.

She would sometimes comment to friends that Jason was now the best thing in her life, and, although she wisely took great care not to overly mother him, the two of them were remarkably close. Jason had once been rather embarrassed when he happened to overhear one of his mother's friends remark: "I envy you your son; he's so kind and thoughtful!"
......

It was only a short bicycle ride to Jason's home in the suburb of Bearwood, about three miles northwest of the University, but today he was travelling by bus because he was wearing his one and only suit and wanted to arrive looking reasonable presentable.

Living at home had its pros and cons, but his mother was delighted to have a man in the house, even though he often worked late, and it had limited the size of his student debt. The latter had also been helped by the fact that his excellent undergraduate degree had secured a coveted Research Council studentship to cover his time as a postgraduate research student.

......

It was on the bus going home that, quite out of the blue, Jason suddenly remembered the four splendid – if rather wet – days spent hiking the 96-mile West Highland Way from Glasgow to Fort William with a student friend about three years before. This gave him a brilliant idea.

"I know!" he thought excitedly. "I'll start my holiday by running non-stop up the northern half of the Highland Way. A day of really intensive running should blow the cobwebs away."

The idea of running considerably more than a marathon distance over hilly ground would have sounded ludicrous to anybody who did not know him, but was a consequence of his passion for cross-country running. Not that this was easy to do when living in a Birmingham suburb. However, about once a week, he would cycle out into the countryside to run at least 15 miles in one of his favourite locations and, more often, could be found participating in the training and other events organized by the University's Athletics & Cross Country Club.

"I could follow that by doing some climbing and fell running further into the western Highlands: perhaps even on Skye. Mum might let me take the old camper van to save on accommodation costs; after all, I keep it roadworthy and make sure it passes its MOT!" he continued enthusiastically as he walked the short distance home from the bus stop.

The elderly vehicle in question was only used for occasional day trips now, but his mother was reluctant to part with it because it reminded her of the happy times the three of them had enjoyed on holiday in various parts of the country.

The ideas kept flowing. "If I use the van, I could drive up to Fort William, book a couple of nights at a campsite and sleep there overnight before getting an early train south to somewhere like Tyndrum, and then run back. If it proves a bit too far, there's a shortcut near the end of the West Highland Way that misses out Glen Nevis."

In a happy frame of mind, Jason put his key in the front door lock, the stressful examination almost forgotten.

......

"How did it go?" a voice called from the kitchen. "The kettle's on."

"I passed, thankfully, although it was quite an ordeal!" Jason called back as he removed his shoes – they were not allowed on the living room carpet or upstairs.

His mother rushed out to give him a delighted hug. "Well done, I knew you'd be successful," she said. "When can I address you as Dr Williamson?"

"Never, I hope! Anyway, the title can only be used after the Chancellor has actually conferred the degree at one of the graduation ceremonies," he replied cheerfully. "However, this Doctor would love a cup of tea!"

Chapter 2: Elise

Nearly 250 miles away in a bedsit in Glasgow, Elise rejoiced over the letter just opened; it contained the formal offer of the post of staff nurse at Glasgow Royal Infirmary, commencing in a month's time on the first of July. She had only completed the final examination of her nursing degree at Glasgow University a few days before and been on tenterhooks about the outcome. Had she spent too much time race training with the University Athletic Club, she kept wondering?

However, all was well and she almost bubbled over with excitement at the good news. Not only that, but she would be able to live with her boyfriend, a garage mechanic, in a one-bedroom flat somewhere in the suburbs of the city, especially if he managed to get his hoped-for promotion.

Apart from accepting the nursing post with alacrity, all she needed to do now was to think of some way of celebrating and unwinding after all her hard work.

"I could do some hiking and running in the Trossachs for a few days if I can manage to find some cheap hostels," she thought. "Or what about going up the West Highland Way to Fort William and beyond?"

She had kept herself extremely fit, despite of the heavy workload of a student nurse, having taken part in as many Athletic Club training sessions as she could fit into her tight schedule. The 5,000m race was her speciality and she was currently one of the top two female athletes for this event in the University.

Elise began planning her holiday. In the end, she decided against the more familiar Trossachs and felt drawn towards the relative novelty of trail running over the higher ground towards Fort William and beyond. Looking back nostalgically, she recalled the time when she and a couple of teenage friends had stayed in a small guesthouse at Bridge of Orchy. The weather had not been very good but their hikes had been wonderful: at least so they seemed as she remembered them five years later.

This time, however, if she was going to move from one hostel to another, it would be necessary to severely limit her gear to what could be carried in a modest rucksack.

"The West Highland Way passes through Bridge of Orchy; in fact we hiked on parts of it," she recalled. "There's a station there on the railway line from Glasgow to Fort William."

She opened her laptop to find out what other stations were on or near the West Highland Way and soon found Tyndrum, another village she vaguely remembered, five miles south of Bridge of Orchy. "And Google Maps highlights the Real Food Café – just the place for a celebration breakfast if I can get a really early train tomorrow and spend most of my first day in the great outdoors!"

She consulted the National Rail website and saw that the first train from Queen Street Station was at 05:20 and scheduled to arrive in Tyndrum just over two hours later. "Early to bed then," she promised herself, not at all put off by the time; after all, she was accustomed to the first dayshift in a hospital ward commencing very early.

The train would take a surprisingly long time to cover what was a relatively short distance, but, once north of Dumbarton, the scenery would get progressively better and make the journey itself enjoyable.

......

Elise spent the afternoon getting ready for her adventure. David might be a little annoyed that she was going somewhere without him, but he hated hiking and, anyway, would not be able to take the time off work. If truth be known, she was also a little cross with him.

Only a few weeks before, she had been rather horrified to discover that she was pregnant. As soon as he heard, David had pushed her towards an early abortion, strongly hinting that their future together might depend on it. Unable to bear the thought of losing him, she had agreed. In order to get everything over quickly, he had even paid for the procedure to be done medically in a private clinic.

Now, over a month later, she felt a twinge of guilt. She should at least have contacted her parents in Normandy, where her French mother and Scottish father ran a small nursing home. She loved them dearly and knew full well that they, devout Roman Catholics, believed that abortion was a sin in the eyes of God. Although they had reluctantly accepted by now that their only daughter lacked faith, they would, no doubt, have tried to argue that a nurse, whose mission was to tend the sick, should protect the nascent life in her own body.

So it was, even in the midst of her present happiness, she could not help feeling guilty and hoped that an energetic few days of complete contrast would help her forget.

......

Eight o'clock the following morning saw Elise tucking into a splendid cooked breakfast in the recently opened Real Food Café, accompanied by several cups of weak tea.

She had just finished eating when her smartphone emitted its characteristic little jingle. She picked it up and saw that it was David calling.

"Hallo David," she said cheerfully. "How are things with you this lovely morning?"

A few seconds later, the smile drained from her face.

Chapter 3: Dreams Shattered

Elise visibly wilted as she took the 'phone away from her ear and stared at it in disbelief, almost as if the device itself was responsible for the words just spoken.

Her hand trembled as she lifted the offending object to her cheek again. "David... you can't... mean that," she whispered between quiet sobs. "I only went through with the... uh... procedure because you made it a condition... of us staying together."

The reply cut through her heart like a knife: "It was good while it lasted but I've met someone else..."

The smartphone began to slip from her hand and it was only reflex action that saved it from crashing to the floor. Within the space of a few seconds, her happiness had been shattered, leaving her numb with shock and grief.

An icy hand gripped her heart as one thing became clear through the fog of anguish. It was something she had begun to faintly suspect but kept pushing away because she was so besotted: David had never truly loved her. Maybe he was already eyeing pastures new even whilst pressing for the abortion.

To make matters even worse, Elise's earlier sense of guilt was growing rapidly and adding to the horrible mix churning around inside her. Feeling physically sick, she gripped the edge of the table hard with both hands. Life was no longer worth living. For one terrible moment, she contemplated the unthinkable.

Then, to her great surprise, the buzz and clatter of the busy café faded and in the cocoon of silence that followed she became aware of an indefinable Presence. Suicide was no longer an option; it was as if the concept was so totally incompatible with this Presence that even the merest thought had been forced to flee.

Complete silence reigned for a moment or two. Then she was conscious of a breath of fragrant air flowing over her head, leaving the benediction "Peace...", so soft it was hardly spoken, lingering in its wake. In the silence that followed she was conscious that something indefinable had occurred in the depth of her being. On the surface, however, she still felt awful.

Gradually the sounds of the outside world returned. Gripping the edge of the table hard, Elise tried to puzzle out what had just happened. Who had spoken to her? If the whole strange experience was not a figment of an overactive imagination, it must have some relevance to her plight.

But she could provide no answer and so grabbed the rucksack from the chair beside her and hurried to the toilet to mop up her tears; people were beginning to stare.

......

It was now eight-fifty on a lovely sunny morning, but Elise was oblivious to all that and crossed the main road with no more than a cursory glance. A minute later, she found herself standing outside a convenience store advertising itself as a Mini-Market. She recognized it as the place where she and her friends had bought their lunchtime snacks after hiking down from Bridge of Orchy five years before. She now recalled that the narrow lane beside the store marked the northbound entrance to the West Highland Way.

Desperate to escape, she began to run up the lane. Perhaps she could somehow exorcize her agony and guilt by driving her body to exhaustion.

......

It was only because Elise and her friends had hiked up and down the path more than once that she only made one error before eventually finding herself on the eastern side of the railway line at Bridge of Orchy station. Passing through the subway under the track, she ran on through the hamlet and crossed the A82 road beside a large white hotel.

She was only carrying a single water bottle made of semi-transparent polyester and it was already almost empty. Now able to think slightly more coherently, she was tempted to go inside the hotel to refill it, but the establishment looked rather posh and she could not face the thought of meeting people. Continuing on down a narrow track beside the hotel to the River Orchy, she crossed the ancient bridge that gives the village its name.

Under normal circumstances, she would have delighted to gaze over the parapet in both directions, as she had done years before with her friends, but she was far too miserable today and ploughed on along a series of tracks and paths, even jogging up a steep hill before dropping down towards the remote Inveroran Hotel close to Loch Tulla. Here she did risk slipping inside and finding somewhere to replenish her meagre water supply.

There followed a seven-mile slog up a winding path through a remote but beautiful landscape – if only she had been in a fit state to appreciate it – and climbing almost 250m in the process. At the top, she stopped for a short rest.

To her left, the Glencoe massif, an impressive cluster of peaks, guarded the eastern end of Glen Coe. Directly ahead, the tiny ribbon of the A82 made its way in a wide westerly arc towards the famous Glen. Some distance beyond the road, a line of more modest mountains formed an attractive backdrop.

Everything seemed so tranquil in the sunshine that, for the first time since leaving Tyndrum, Elise became aware of the beauty around her and relaxed ever so slightly. Nevertheless, the burden she carried was still just as heavy and so she scrambled on down the slope towards the road.

The narrow track soon joined a lane running down to the main road. On the other side, a less well-defined path recommenced its journey north. Elise hesitated and then entered – she certainly did not fancy staying on the busy road – and jogged on.

She was now beyond the area explored with her teenage friends, but, having spent a short time the previous afternoon on the Walk Highlands website noting some of the landmarks and twists and turns on the way to Fort William, she was not surprised to come across the Kings House Hotel, seemingly sitting in the middle of nowhere.

Even though there were a surprising number of cars outside, she plucked up the courage to slip inside. After visiting the cloakroom and topping up her bottle, the idea of something else to drink appealed, but the bar was busy and so she hurriedly escaped.

......

The West Highland Way went north along one of the access routes to the hotel and joined a track running west towards Glen Coe. Elise began to run rather blindly down the smooth surface until, after about a mile, the track suddenly emerged on the A82. She had failed to spot the entrance to an earlier path that climbs to slightly higher ground and enables hikers on the Way to avoid the busy road.

Aware that it was necessary to go further west before climbing over the formidable ridge bounding the northern side of Glen Coe, she began jogging rather precariously along the narrow verge. Fortunately, about a mile later, the path missed earlier appeared on her right and ran beside the road.

It was not long before the path crossed a pedestrian bridge spanning a small stream and curved sharp right to begin climbing the slope. A brown finger post stood at the corner bearing the reassuring words "West Highland Way" written vertically in white letters under a thistle between two chevrons.

"So this is the entrance to the Devil's Staircase," Elise muttered, viewing the path as it snaked up the slope before disappearing into the heather. "I've got to climb 250m over the next mile and then scramble down over twice that to reach Kinlochleven at sea level," she recalled from the previous afternoon's research.

The climb became much steeper over the second half mile where the path zigzagged up the slope and frequently literally took the form of a rocky staircase.

Jogging uphill for so long, even very slowly, is completely draining, but Elise was tough and grimly determined to do it, however much it hurt. Nevertheless, it took everything she had to reach the two stone cairns marking the top of the pass.

She sagged against one of them and struggled to extract her water bottle from the net pocket at the side of her pack. There was very little water left by the time she moved on.

"I'll fill up in Kinlochleven," she promised herself. Unfortunately, she failed to do so.

......

Meanwhile, on the day previous to Elise's departure from Glasgow, Jason had driven all the way north from Birmingham and parked the campervan in a caravan park just outside Fort William after paying the fee for two nights. He was certainly ready for an early night but treated himself to a modest meal in a nearby restaurant before retiring to one of the narrow bunks. To his surprise, he slept quite well and was not aware of waking again until his small alarm buzzed close to his ear at six o'clock.

The first train south that morning was at 7:44 but it stopped so many times that Jason was not in Tyndrum until almost one and a half hours later. It was only a short walk to the centre of the village. On spying the Real Food Café, he had the sudden urge to pop in for a quick cup of coffee before setting out to run back to Fort William. He had sensibly decided to omit the detour that the West Highland Way takes to Glen Nevis shortly before the finish.

"Almost forty miles is not a bad challenge for my first day!" he thought as he sipped the coffee. "If I leave here by ten, I should be able to get back well before dark, although it's lucky I remembered to bring a head torch just in case. After Kinlochleven, twelve miles from Fort William, there's nowhere to shelter!"

He set out in high spirits, rejoicing in the early June sunshine tempered by a gentle breeze. "It's good to be alive!" he thought and only just stopped himself proclaiming the fact aloud to a couple of approaching hikers. Nevertheless, they looked quite surprised when he passed them with a joyful "Good Morning!"

In his happy frame of mind it seemed no time at all before Bridge of Orchy was behind him, although he had paused for several minutes to take in the views from the bridge whilst sipping from one of his water bottles. It was not until he was jogging across the high ground between the Black Mount cluster and Loch Tulla, now far below, that he began to notice his aching muscles.

"Perhaps I'm not as fit as I thought!" he surmised, before recalling that finalizing his dissertation and preparing for the oral examination had made significant inroads into his time for athletic activities.

"Anyway, I'm determined to push on through the pain barrier and keep hydrated," he promised himself.

He was thankful his mother had thought to remind him to take a tube of electrolyte tablets just as he was hurriedly leaving home on the long drive north. When planning a run of more than ten miles, he was accustomed to dissolving a tablet contained vitamin C, sodium, magnesium and potassium in one of the two water bottles he carried.

He ploughed on, aided by the anticipation of a quick pit stop at the Kings House Hotel.

......

Jason had to battle the pain barrier in real earnest when he was jogging slowly up the Devil's Staircase. He was determined not to stop and give way to the burning sensation in his leg muscles and, almost as bad, aching joints. The unfamiliar scenery had helped to distract him earlier, but, as the burning got worse, this was no longer working and so he tried puzzling over one of the many cosmic conundrums encountered in his research. This worked quite well for a time, although he had to keep an eye on the rough path.

He was grateful for the relatively stress-free descent into Kinlochleven. Shortly after crossing the River Leven, the West Highland Way followed a well-maintained path along the north bank of the river for a short distance before coming out on the B863 in the centre of the village. Immediately opposite was the welcome sight of the Tailrace Inn.

"Time for a pit stop," he breathed thankfully.

......

But time was passing quickly and so, not much more than half an hour later, Jason was beginning the steep climb northwest up a narrow path through a dense wood. The mile-long path rose about 240m in long zigzags. Determined to maintain a slow jog, he focussed on his breathing, trying not to gasp but breathe in deeply and then exhale as fully as possible. This not only helped to increase his oxygen supply but acted as something of a distraction from the pain.

At last the gradient eased and the path merged with a much wider track. "Part of one of the old military roads used to move soldiers around Scotland centuries ago," he recalled from information gleaned from the Walk Highland website. "This one leads all the way to Fort William. In a few miles it'll all be downhill!" His jogging speed improved as if in celebration; journey's end was in sight – at least almost.

It was well into the evening and the few people encountered earlier had all been returning to Kinlochleven. Thus Jason was quite surprised to see a tall girl about fifty yards ahead going in the direction of Fort William. But her movements were extremely odd; in fact, she was stumbling from side to side rather alarmingly.

Realizing she was in trouble, Jason speeded up and rapidly closed the gap. "I hope she's not drunk," he muttered anxiously.

Chapter 4: The Good Samaritan

Elise was in real trouble by the time she reached the old military road high above Kinlochleven. All her muscles were burning and she was getting frequent spasms of cramp. Even worse, her fatigue was such that she kept fading out for a second or two and then being too dazed to remember where she was. All she knew was that she must struggle onwards.

Taking another desperate step, her foot caught on a stone and she pitched forward, only to be caught by a strong arm before she hit the ground.

"It's OK, I've got you," a distant voice said.

As if in a dream, she found herself being half carried a short distance off the track and lowered to sit on a rock.

"You need water," the voice said, now clearer.

She was vaguely conscious of someone tapping her empty water bottle. Then she felt an arm supporting her from behind and an unfamiliar bottle pressed gently to her lips.

"This is orange flavoured water with some minerals added," the voice said. "Drink slowly and then I'll give you some plain water."

Now conscious of her extreme thirst, Elise clasped the bottle with both hands and gulped greedily.

"Not so fast! Let your body absorb it gradually." A firm hand restrained her eagerness for a moment or two and then let her drink again before taking the bottle away altogether. It was soon replaced by another. "Sip this water slowly. There's no hurry."

"Actually, there is," Jason thought. "We're still ten miles from Fort William. If she only recovers enough to walk slowly, it could be midnight before we get there. I can't risk taking her back a mile and then down the very steep path into Kinlochleven in her present state."

He looked at the girl with concern, wondering why someone who was wearing sensible running gear and appeared to be strong and athletic could have been foolish enough to get so badly dehydrated. Then he had a flash of insight; she was in this distressed state because she was running away from someone or something.

To his great relief, the girl opened her eyes fully for the first time and turned to look at him. "I'm sorry to have used up so much of your water," she said apologetically. "I'm ashamed of myself for getting in this state. I received some terrible news this morning just as I was setting out on a short running holiday. In my overwrought state, I suppose I thought some punishing exercise might help to mitigate the anguish."

She lapsed into silence after having revealed so much to a stranger, but he had rescued her and she could not help noticing his sympathetic smile and kind eyes.

Jason smiled again and held out his hand. "I'm Jason and on my way to Fort William."

The girl gave him a smile that lit up her strained face. "I'm Elise. Thank you for all your help. I suppose I'm aiming for the youth hostel in Fort William, although my original idea was to do the trip in two or three days before venturing somewhere further north."

"Then we can carry on along this track together at whatever speed you feel able to manage," Jason replied.

Elise looked relieved that he was going to stay with her. The water and minerals were working wonders but she was still sore and felt extremely fragile. She wobbled slightly as she stood to her feet but managed to walk with Jason supporting her elbow.

It was not long before he hesitantly asked permission to hold her hand so that they could swing their arms and keep their balance more easily on the rough surface. Elise was surprised to discover how comforting this felt.

In fact, there was something so encouraging about Jason's presence at her side, ready to assist if she stumbled, that her aches and pains faded somewhat and she began to feel considerably better. It was not long, therefore, before she suggested speeding up and they were soon covering the ground more quickly, helped by the fact that they were now on almost level ground.

Just over half a mile later they came to a derelict stone cottage with no roof. It had two doorways and three chimney stacks and so Jason surmised that it was probably the remains of two crofters' dwellings. There was a convenient stone and concrete platform outside one empty threshold and he made Elise sit down for another short drink of his precious water. He would have to do without because her need was much greater than his.

They continued to jog slowly west through a glen that appeared almost magical in the glow of the setting sun, its rays just clipping the top of one of the low peaks and causing a multitude of shapes and shadows to appear on the flank of the opposite ridge. There was a wonderful sense of tranquillity.

Elise recalled the word "Peace" breathed over her in the midst of her agony in the café. It had seemed the complete antithesis of what she was experiencing then, but now she felt enfolded in peace on every side, so much so that her inner anguish began to subside.

"Let's try jogging faster," she found herself saying.

"Of course, if you feel up to it," Jason said in surprised relief.

It greatly helped when the track turned northwest and began a slow two-mile descent to merge with a narrow lane that joined them from the left. The surface was now much smoother and easier on the feet. It did not take long, therefore, before they passed the point at which the West Highland Way left the lane to go northeast towards Glen Nevis.

Jason pointed ahead. "We're now on the direct route to Fort William."

......

They jogged on, Elise quite surprised that she was able to keep going despite her aching limbs. "I suppose I'm basically pretty strong and fit after all my race training. Today was only a near disaster because of my terrible frame of mind and stupid neglect," she concluded.

They were now passing fields and small buildings with frequent views of Loch Linnhe not far away. However, it was rapidly getting dark and she realized that the hostel, wherever it was, would almost certainly be closed by the time she got there.

Jason appeared to have read her thoughts because he stopped to unbuckle his rucksack and extract his head torch before handing Elise the bottle with the remaining liquid.

She shook it: there was very little left. "You haven't had any since you rescued me!" she objected.

"No problem; I was well hydrated before we met," he said before continuing quickly. "I've no idea where the hostel is, but it's almost certainly closed by now and only registered guests will have a key. I've a spare bunk in my camper van if you'd like to crash out there for the night. I can even give you some much needed soup with bread and cheese."

Elise looked at him, her eyes wide. "You really are a Good Samaritan; in fact, all that's missing are the robbers who beat me up! Anyway, thank you for being so kind."

Jason just managed to catch the smile she gave him in the glow of his torch and it warmed his heart. "You're very welcome," he said before thoughtlessly adding: "In a sense, you were been beaten up – by that bad news you mentioned."

He immediately regretted his tactless remark but, thankfully, Elise did not seem to have noticed.

......

They reached the extensive suburbs of Fort William spread out along the bank of Loch Linnhe. Occasional street lamps now lit their passage.

"The caravan park is north of the railway station, unfortunately, and so it'll still take us nearly half an hour to get there," Jason said apologetically.

"Never mind, your kind offer has cheered me up no end – I was beginning to worry about lack of accommodation. I certainly can't afford an upmarket hotel!"

They jogged slowly on. Both were now extremely weary and Elise only managed to keep going by concentrating on keeping close to her companion.

......

At long last, Jason guided her into the entrance to what was obviously a caravan park: mobile homes lined one side of the service road and several caravans and campervans were dotted about in parking slots set in an area of grass on the opposite side.

"Here we are," Jason said, leading her to a rather elderly vehicle and unlocking the rear doors. "This van has a cold water tank and is connected to electricity. There's also a small chemical toilet but for proper washing etc. we need to go to that building over there." He nodded in the appropriate direction.

Elise smiled gratefully; a shower might have to wait until tomorrow, but she was beginning to need the other facilities.

"You go first, there are warm-air hand driers but I'll give you my spare towel if you need it when you go for a shower," he said.

Elise thanked him as she removed her rucksack and extracted a small sponge bag before departing.

......

When she returned, the soup was already warming on the bottled-gas stove and two glasses of water together with bread, butter and cheese were laid out on a narrow table between the single bunks that lined the sides of the van. The delicious smell reminded her how famished she was.

"Start as soon as the soup is hot. The burner control is rather tricky, so leave it on if you have difficulty. I won't be long," Jason said as he hurried off.

......

By the time they had eaten, it was well after midnight and the young couple were too tired to contemplate showers; even the firm narrow bunk looked inviting after Jason had folded the table away and produced sheets, pillows and thin duvets from an overhead storage locker.

Elise fell into an exhausted sleep almost as soon as her head touched the pillow. Jason looked down at her wonderingly just before he turned the lights out; she looked so young and vulnerable as she lay there with a shadow of sadness on her weary face.

"She's clearly been through something very unpleasant. I'm glad she trusts me. Perhaps we were meant to meet. I'm determined to help in any way I can." Thoughts such as these passed through his mind as he lay down.

He was also asleep within minutes, but, unusually for him, had several quite vivid dreams during the night. They all involved Elise and seemed to have something to do with Skye, which was strange because he had never visited that island.

……

A late night meant that they did not rouse until shortly after eight o'clock. Showers helped to make a late cooked breakfast all the more enjoyable.

Jason looked at Elise as she tucked in hungrily. The aura of sadness still remained, but, physically, she had made a remarkable recovery. In his eyes at least, she had a near-perfect runner's physique and looked extremely attractive in charcoal shorts and sleeveless top that revealed her firmly muscled arms and legs.

He plucked up the courage to issue an invitation. "I don't know where you were planning to go after Fort William but you'd be more than welcome to come with me to Skye if you can cope with the narrow bunk – and me of course! I've made rough plans to stop at a couple of campsites, one in Broadford, about seven miles from Kyle of Lochalsh, and the other in the north of the island. What do you think?"

Elise gazed at him for what seemed like minutes but was only a few seconds. Then she gave him a wondering smile. "Can you really put up with me in my miserable state?" she asked. "If so, I'd love to come; I've never been to Skye but have heard that parts are wild and beautiful. Something like that might act as a sort of healing balm."

"That's settled then," Jason beamed at her. "I suggest we walk into the centre to do a little shopping before tidying up in here. We have to leave this pitch by midday."

Chapter 5: Destination Skye

Just before twelve o'clock, Jason drove the camper van out of Fort William and northeast up the A82 towards Inverness.

"We're about to enter the southern end of the Great Glen and go about twenty miles to Invergarry where we'll join the A87 and head northwest," he said. "The A87 winds its way through the mountains for fifty miles to Kyle of Lochalsh, then crosses Skye Bridge and runs all the way up the eastern side of the island to its northern tip. The bridge was only opened in 1995; before that there was a ferry."

The view was frequently obscured by thick trees and it was not until they were well past Spean Bridge that the Great Glen narrowed and it was possible to appreciate the enclosing mountains. The road now followed the eastern bank of an attractive stretch of water.

"That's Loch Lochy; the famous Loch Ness is further up," Jason commented when he saw Elise's interest.

She gave a contented little sigh and wriggled slightly as if snuggling back in the passenger seat. "All this is completely new to me," she said.

"Then it's new to both of us and I'm glad you're enjoying it," Jason replied softly.

She glanced at his profile. "He's not just being polite; he really is glad!" she thought in amazement before saying aloud: "Do tell me something about yourself."

......

They were quite a way along the westbound road before Jason finished giving a potted version of his life. It had taken longer than expected because of Elise's fascination with his research.

"I think you're very clever!" she said as they reached the end of a splendid stretch of road beside Loch Cluanie and pulled into the car park of an attractive white building appropriately named Cluanie Inn.

"Thanks for the compliment but it was mainly the result of perseverance and hard work," Jason replied with a chuckle. "Anyway, it's time for a pit-stop!"

......

They set off again forty minutes later but had only driven about ten miles when Jason spotted a garage. "I'd better fill up here; it'll probably be cheaper than on Skye."

Elise quickly opened the passenger door and sprang out. "You fill up; I'll pay inside. After all, I'm getting a free bed in the van!" she declared and disappeared inside before he had time to argue.

They crossed a narrow river immediately after leaving the garage. "That's the Sheil – it runs into Loch Duich, the first of the two sea lochs on the route to Skye," Jason volunteered.

Rounding a bend, they drove through a cutting in the rock and Loch Duich lay before them. "It's surprisingly big," Elise remarked.

Jason nodded. "Yes, and we'll soon turn northwest again to follow its northern shore for roughly five miles."

The old camper van purred along at a modest speed giving Elise a splendid view of the attractive loch through her side window.

"It's really lovely here!" she exclaimed at one point. "And is that a castle up there on the left overlooking the water?"

"Yes; according to Google Maps it's Eilean Donan Castle," Jason said. "There's been a fortification there for at least seven hundred years. The original structure is thought to have been built to defend the coast against the Vikings."

They soon passed the entrance of a large car park with the Castle beyond – although not much was visible from the road – and crossed a bridge spanning the channel connecting Loch Duich with the southern end of Loch Long.

"The Castle was in the strategic position to defend the entrances of both lochs from an enemy sailing up Loch Alsh from the open sea," Jason explained. "We're now about to bear west along the northern shore of Loch Alsh for the eight miles to Kyle of Lochalsh."

Despite ominous clouds gathering in the west, the views were still impressive, especially when the road ran beside the water, only separated from it by a safety barrier and narrow band of grass and bushes. Eventually, they rounded a bend and there, silhouetted against the dull sky, a graceful arc spanned the strait between the mainland and the legendary island.

"Skye Bridge!" Elise exclaimed, sounding quite excited.

Jason smiled, pleased at her reaction; the journey was clearly helping to distract her from her problems but he realized it would take time. At least twice on the trip so far he had spotted her staring directly ahead with the set of her lower lip and telltale crease on her cheek conveying a deep sense of sorrow.

"I'm determined to do everything I can to help her get over this crisis in her life, whatever it is," he promised himself.

......

They had barely left the viaduct linking the mainland to the tiny island of Eilean Ban and begun the climb over the 500m bridge, when the storm broke. The van swayed in a strong gust of wind and Jason hurriedly switched on the windscreen wipers and lights.

"Sorry about this," he said as he peered forward anxiously through the torrent. He was loath to slow down too much in case someone ran into the back of the van.

Fortunately, the wind was less when they reached land again but the rain continued almost unabated for the few miles it took to reach the campsite on the outskirts of Broadford. They both breathed a sigh of relief when Jason finally backed into the space allocated to them and switched off the engine.

"Thank you for cleverly managing to book a pitch fairly near the shower block," Elise said.

"I wasn't offered any choice!" Jason replied.

Chapter 6: Camasunary Bay

Elise and Jason's first full day on Skye dawned with the early promise of sunshine. The curtains in the van were thin and light was flooding in by five o'clock in the morning. Having gone to bed early the previous evening, Elise was already preparing breakfast an hour later while Jason was having a shower. He returned to the delicious smell of bacon and eggs.

"I thought we needed a nourishing meal before setting out on today's adventure," she said as she laid his plate on the table.

Outwardly, she looked ready for anything, but her cheerfulness had a brittle edge and Jason was astute enough to detect that she was still struggling to overcome whatever had caused her to get in such a sad state only two days earlier.

Realizing that he had been gazing at her for longer than was polite, he said quickly: "I'm glad you appear to have had a good night on an uncomfortable bunk. As for something scenic and hopefully adventurous, I suggest taking the van south down the B8083 to Kilmarie, just over ten miles from here, and hike to Camasunary Bay and back. The Skye website highly recommends it; the scenery is beautiful and the beach well worth a visit.... This breakfast is excellent by the way!"

Elise joined him at the table with their mugs of tea and nodded. "An energetic hike on a day like this is just what's needed after yesterday's journey. I'll make some sandwiches for a picnic on the beach. Do you want an apple or a banana?"

"Banana please, and I'll find the thermos flask."

......

Jason carefully parked the campervan just south of Kilmarie in the dedicated lay-by for the Camasunary walk and shouldered the rucksack containing their refreshments.

"You should have let me carry something," Elise reiterated as they crossed the road and entered a gravel track that wound its way up a valley of coarse grass and heather.

"No; I wanted you to be free to enjoy yourself without encumbrance," Jason replied, trying to avoid getting his trainers wet in a large puddle almost completely blocking their passage. "Not surprising in view of all yesterday's rain," he added with a chuckle.

Soon the gravel was party replaced by large stones of varying size. In places the latter had been laid to make what had once been a good surface, but the combination of time, elements and the passage of four-wheeled vehicles had caused considerable deterioration.

A narrow stream cut across the path. Jason watched as Elise ignored the stepping stones and sprang effortlessly across. "She's a superb athlete as well as a pleasure to be with," he thought. Was he falling in love? All he knew for certain was that he had never enjoyed a girl's company so much.

The track levelled off for a short distance before slowly climbing again. The tops of several distant mountains appeared over the brow of the ridge ahead.

"This is splendid!" Elise breathed, almost to herself.

Secretly, she was surprised that she was feeling so buoyant despite her inner heaviness. She had put on a cheerful face at breakfast because she was determined not to spoil Jason's much-needed holiday, but now the sun, fresh air and beautiful scenery were having a remarkable effect, not to mention her love of exercise. On top of all this was something she hardly dared admit to herself: there was something special about Jason.

……

The young couple encountered more wet patches, puddles and streams before reaching a kissing-gate, after which the track narrowed even further to commence a long winding climb on stones that had, in places, been mortared in position to prevent slippage.

They passed a carefully constructed cairn of small stones, presumably intended to mark the way in bad weather because the crest of the ridge was some distance away. More mountain peaks appeared and there were occasional glimpses of water. All this piqued Elise's interest and she pressed on eagerly.

Finally they reached the crest of the 150m ridge. A long range of mountains stood proudly in the far west, no longer screened by the lower hills. The sea was now in view to the south and, beyond, the faint outline of distant islands.

"Wow!" said Elise as she surveyed the scene. Jason took her arm affectionately as he stood beside her. "Those are the Cuillins," he said. "Some are over 900m high."

They followed the path along the crest of the ridge but it was only when starting on the long winding descent that they caught the first tantalizing glimpses of the beach. Then, at last, the whole of Camasunary Bay was spread out before them.

"Thank you so much for bringing me here!" Elise cried.

In a moment of enthusiasm, she took Jason's hand. It was only for a few seconds but caused his whole body to tingle.

They eagerly tackled the remainder of descent, the breathtaking scenery and bright sunshine combining to instil a sense of anticipation and adventure.

Nearing the bottom, they crossed a rickety bridge and were surprised to see two white houses standing in a meadow of coarse grass a short distance inland from the water.

"Surely people don't live in this remote spot," Elise remarked.

"Well it would explain the vehicle tracks further back. Even with a four-wheel drive you might be cut off in the winter," Jason said before guiding her off the track and down a grassy path towards the water.

The foreshore was entirely composed of grey gravel, but the tide was on the ebb and an inviting stretch of greyish sand and small stones lay below a narrow band of seaweed.

"What's that tiny building?" Elise asked, pointing to the far end of the bay.

"I think it must be the bothy mentioned on the website. Hikers can shelter there in bad weather or even camp at night," Jason told her. "Anyway, we can have our lunch when we get there."

"I'm hungry. Let's run on the sand," Elise said, striding over the shingle and then turning to face him with a cheeky grin. "I bet I can beat you to the end of the beach."

"In your dreams!" Jason replied in similar vein. "But first let me tighten the straps of this rucksack."

A few seconds later, they were crouching side by side. "One, two, three, go!" Elise cried and they were off, neck and neck to start with, but it was not long before Jason found out just how good a runner his companion was.

Her feet literally seemed to fly across the smooth surface and she gradually pulled ahead by at least three metres. He had to pull out all the stops to prevent the gap widening further, but after covering 500 yards or so, and sensing he was still on her heels, she put on a final sprint that sealed her victory. Stopping near the bank of a small river that was flowing into the sea, she turned to face him with a cry of triumph.

Jason came to a stop beside her. "You're a terrific runner. I thought I was fit but you're amazing," he gasped.

"Well, you were carrying the rucksack. Also, don't forget, my speciality is the 5,000m track event, not tens of kilometres over rough country like you," Elise said generously.

On impulse she took his hand again and they walked the short distance over the grass to the white bothy. It was larger than they had expected but dark and gloomy inside. Jason therefore extracted his anorak from the rucksack so that they could sit outside on the damp grass overlooking the sea. It was a tight squeeze for both of them but he certainly did not mind.

All too soon it was time to leave the beautiful beach and so, rather regretfully, the two young people clambered up the winding track to the top of the ridge before stopping to look back. "I must remember this place and come again sometime," Elise said softly.

"It certainly rates a return visit," Jason agreed, but could not help thinking that her presence had made everything so much better. He recalled, that, on the long drive to Fort William, he had begun to regret rushing off in such a hurry that there had been no time to find a friend to accompany him, but now, of course, he was thankful he had come alone. It was almost as if providence – if indeed there was such a thing – had provided the ideal companion at just the right moment.

They moved on and descended as far as the stone cairn before stopping for a drink.

As Elise was handing her water bottle back to Jason, a flash of light caught her eye; something shiny was lying a few feet away partly obscured by a clump of heather. She moved over and discovered a plastic sleeve containing what appeared to be a blank white postcard. One edge was damp and she guessed that it had probably been there overnight, if not longer.

She turned the card over and saw some words printed in bold type: "Bible Treasure Hunt – St. John, Ch.14, v.27".

"I wonder what a Bible Treasure Hunt is," she pondered.

"I guess a number of similar cards were semi-hidden close to the path recently and then some children or teenagers set out to find and record as many as they could find on a score sheet. There was probably a prize of some sort for the one who discovered the most verses," he surmised. "The cards must have been collected up afterwards; if not, we would have spotted one before now."

But Elise was not listening: she was transfixed by the verse itself. "Peace I leave with you; my peace I give you. I do not give as the world gives. Do not let your hearts be troubled and do not be afraid," it stated.

"This is… astonishing," she whispered. Then she turned to Jason, her eyes full of tears. "You remember I told you it was while having breakfast in Tyndrum that I received the news that so upset me?" she said slowly. Jason nodded.

"Well," she continued, "what I didn't tell you was that, immediately afterwards, when I was feeling totally desperate, all the sounds in the café faded and I was surrounded by complete silence. Although I saw nothing, I sensed someone standing beside me and I distinctly heard the word "Peace" spoken over me like some sort of benediction. After a few moments the normal sounds returned and I was alone again with my misery. The experience was quite extraordinary and I had no idea what to make of it, but I'm sure it prevented me from doing something even more drastic than running myself to exhaustion.

"Perhaps finding this quote about peace from the Bible is not a coincidence but has some relevance to my situation. After all, there must have been a lot more cards with different verses on the day of the treasure hunt, but only this one got left behind. But what am I supposed to do about it? I can't just tell myself to snap out of it and feel peaceful about everything when I'm most certainly not!"

Jason was thoughtful for a moment and then took Elise's hand in both of his. "As this quote is from St John's Gospel in the New Testament it must be something Jesus said to his followers. Thus, a Christian would probably say that it was Jesus who spoke to you in the café. The problem for us – or me at least – is that this requires a belief in the supernatural. All I can be fairly certain about is that the word "Peace" can't be a figment of your imagination because, at that moment, you were about as far from peaceful as it's possible to be!"

He paused briefly and then blurted out: "I'm so thankful to have been on the path above Kinlochleven at the right time and run – almost literally – into a very special girl like you."

He blushed, suddenly conscious that this was not the time to reveal his feelings; it was much more important to be ready with a sympathetic listening ear. To his surprise, however, it seemed that his words had been exactly right because Elise was regarding him with a mixture of gratitude and hope on her tear-stained face.

"Thank you for your insight and, above all, your patience and kindness. I feel I can trust you completely. May I tell you what led up to all this and why I was so devastated," she whispered, so quietly that he only just heard her words before they were swept away by the breeze blowing in their faces.

"Of course you may and I promise nothing you share will go any further," he replied as he led her to a small grassy mound not far from the path and spread out his anorak.

......

For the next twenty minutes, Elise poured out her grief, even including her shame at having had an abortion. "So you see, I was so determined to do almost anything to make sure I didn't lose David that I agreed with his suggestion without giving it proper thought or discussing it with my parents. I love them dearly and they will be shocked to say the least. But now I've been cast off by my ex-boyfriend like…," she trailed off into near silence and sat sobbing quietly.

"He must be completely mad to treat you like this," Jason muttered, almost to himself, and then more loudly: "It's awful for you, I know, but at least you know where you stand. It would have been far worse if it had happened after you had married him."

"I suppose so," Elise said rather doubtfully, but then felt his arm around her shoulders. It was so comforting that she rested her head against his shoulder.

"Anyway, I'm determined to help by making sure you have a good holiday," he responded, delighting in her closeness. "We may even find some more clues to your peace conundrum or get a flash of inspiration. I sometimes find it helps to leave a knotty problem at the back of your mind and get on with something else."

Chapter 7: A Splendid Day

After an early evening meal eaten outside the van in the pleasant evening sunshine, Jason invited Elise to stroll down to the village for a drink.

"It's a lovely evening for it," she said dreamily as they walked arm in arm down the main road. "When we drove all the way through Broadford yesterday it didn't appear to have a centre; the buildings are scattered almost randomly along a mile or so of the road."

Then she noticed that they were about to pass an attractive public garden overlooking the sea. "Perhaps this nice garden marks the centre."

Jason nodded. "Especially in view of the car park up there with the Coop store beyond," he said, pointing towards a large building not far ahead on their side of the road.

It was only then that he noticed a small white building with a tiny bell-tower directly opposite them. "Look, that must be a church," he remarked, suddenly feeling the urge to have a closer look. Somewhat to her surprise, Elise found herself being guided across the road.

There were two notice boards: the first listed details of regular church services and the second carried advertisements for local events. But there was one exception. The two young people could not help their attention being drawn to a poster with large white lettering overprinting a beautiful pastoral scene. It was so colourful that they moved over to read what it said.

"Now that we have been put right with God through faith, we have peace with God through our Lord Jesus Christ. He has brought us by faith into this experience of God's grace, in which we now live. (Romans 5: 1-2, GNT)".

Hardly able to believe her eyes, Elise exclaimed: "This is the third time the word "peace" has come up; it really can't be a coincidence!"

"I agree; we'd better write these things down when we get back to the campsite. In the meantime...," Jason's words trailed off as he opened his smartphone and took a picture of the notice board. "Now let's find a pub or something."

"You're an amazing help," Elise said as she linked arms again. A surge of happiness filled him to the core.

......

While the young couple enjoyed a refreshing drink at a table on a terrace overlooking the sea, Jason outlined his suggestions for the following day.

"Tomorrow, weather permitting, you'd probably like to do something more energetic than the relatively short hike we did today," he said, raising his eyebrows enquiringly.

Elise nodded enthusiastically. "By all means; I'm game for anything."

Pleased with her response, he continued: "There's a hiking route known as the Skye Trail that starts in the north of the island and winds all the way down to Broadford. Before leaving home, I discovered that the final section commences in Torrin, a hamlet just over five miles down the B8083. We passed through it today on our way to Kilmarie. The hike is well over twice the distance by road and involves two climbs of 100m or more and some coastal sections. There should be some splendid views, especially of the mountains west of here. I suggest we run down the road from here and then come back along the Trail. By the way, there's said to be a café in Torrin that has very good coffee."

"It's called the Blue Shed. I remember passing it today and thinking how nice it looked," Elise said, giving her companion a warm smile. Despite her nagging sadness, she could not help feeling excited at the thought of the day to come.

......

Running on a single-track road meant that Elise and Jason had to mount the narrow verge every time an occasional vehicle approached, but, whenever there was a clear stretch of road ahead, Elise set a pace that surprised and delighted her companion, who often had to dig deep to keep up. In fact, it was not long before he got the distinct impression that she was enjoying testing him.

"She's a superb runner and must be a formidable opponent in 5,000m road and track events. I'm enjoying every moment spent with her. I'm sure I'm falling in love! But I must be cautious because she's still hurting from her recent experience." These thoughts swirled around in Jason's head as he followed her speeding heels.

After about five miles, Elise slowed to a stop beside a small sign announcing that the outskirts of Torrin had been reached. No dwellings were visible but a large body of water lay ahead.

"That's Loch Slapin; Torrin lies not far from its head," Jason remarked rather breathlessly. He gazed at Elise in admiration. The fast pace had barely dented her vitality and her cheeks glowed delightfully. "You're a superb runner!" he added, handing her a water bottle.

She grinned, clearly pleased with his reaction, but shook her head modestly before saying: "Now lead me to this coffee."

......

After running over half a mile to the northern outskirts of Torrin, the young couple relaxed at a table on the terrace outside the Blue Shed café enjoying the view of Loch Slapin and surrounding mountains.

"The reviews are certainly accurate," Jason murmured contentedly, sipping his excellent coffee. Then he lapsed into silence while he searched for something on his smartphone. "I wonder...," he trailed off.

Intrigued, Elise looked at him with a gentle smile. "Jason's really helping me forget my woes by suggesting these splendid outings. It's so good that we both enjoy the same activities."

If the object of her gaze had glanced up at this point, he would have noticed a sudden look of surprise; it was as if a curtain had been opened and she could view things in a new light. Not only was Jason's presence a marvellous help in overcoming the pain of abandonment, but, for the first time since that awful morning in Tyndrum, her turbulent affair with David was being completely exposed for what it had been all along: self-centred passion between two people with no real love at its core. The young man sitting deep in thought beside her was so totally different from David that there could be no comparison. Whilst he clearly liked her company and delighted in their shared love of running, there had never been anything even remotely salacious in his gaze: only warmth, pleasure and – yes – even joy. He was unconsciously demonstrating true friendship in everything he said and did.

"I think I'm falling in love for real this time!" This conclusion came to her in a flash as Jason looked up with a smile and pointed north towards the mountains rising above the grassy slope on the other side of the road.

"It's barely eleven o'clock and far too early to return to Broadford along the Skye Trail," he said. "Would you like to climb to the top of a 570m mountain? I think it may be the one immediately behind that low hill. Anyway, it's definitely not one of the taller mountains to the right. I've been consulting the Walk Highlands website to see what hikes are recommended near here. Apparently the one up Beinn na Cro has some splendid views, especially on a day like this. What do you think?"

Elise beamed at him. "That's a brilliant idea. A tough climb suits me fine."

"Splendid!" Jason replied. "The path starts at the head of Loch Slapin and so we need to continue up this road for just over a mile. The complete round trip from here is about five miles."

"A mere snip!" she exclaimed. "A picnic lunch on a mountain top: how lovely!"

......

Elise led the way once again and Jason followed her the short distance down to shore of Loch Slapin. Here the narrow road curved sharply right to run northwest beside the water.

About a mile later, as she was approaching a bridge spanning a shallow river feeding the head of the Loch, Jason called for her to stop.

"That must be Beinn na Cro," he said pointing to a relatively modest mountain standing at the entrance of the glen. "You see the wire fence running up the slope there?"

"Yes," Elise nodded.

"Well, the website says that we should follow an indistinct path a few metres to the left of the fence until reaching a stream flowing down from the summit in a shallow ravine or gully. There we have to bear left and climb along the edge of the gully until it comes out on the open ground leading to the summit."

"I think I can see the gully; it just looks like a gash in the hillside from here," Elise said. "The stream must be the one I noticed meandering down the slope and running under the road to join the loch. We passed over it a minute ago."

Jason had been too intent on keeping up with his athletic companion to notice the stream and so he merely said: "The views are splendid down here but they'll get even more spectacular higher up. Let's go!"

Elise beamed at him and they set off full of anticipation, jogging at first but slowing to a brisk climbing pace when the gradient became steeper. Just below the gully, they had a brief water stop and turned to admire the view back over Loch Slapin and the mountains to the west.

A particularly formidable mountain, clearly higher than the one they were climbing, guarded the other side of the entrance to the glen. Jason noticed Elise looking at it with interest, and, glad of the excuse for a short breather, he consulted his 'phone again.

"I think that must be Belig at about 700m," he said. "You can tell it's quite high because the top half is completely bare rock."

"That'd present a serious climb and probably need proper boots but I'd like to try it sometime, or perhaps even one of those higher mountains further to the left!" Elise said.

"The highest in that group is Bla Bheinn at 928m. Apparently the name means Blue Mountain although I can't see anything blue about it," Jason informed her.

Refreshed by the water and short rest, the young couple moved on, soon arriving at the edge of the gully where they paused to watch the stream tumbling down just below them. Bearing left, the real climb of the day began as they carefully followed the ridge upwards.

The views got better and better as they climbed. Elise appeared to be in her element and was enjoying every minute. Climbing either beside or behind her, as the rough indistinct path dictated, Jason rejoiced in her happiness.

The stream gradually petered out and the ridge blended into the shoulder of the mountain not far from the summit. To their left, the ground fell away sharply into the wide glen in which the river threaded its way down to Loch Slapin, gathering water from several tiny lochs on the way.

"This is a splendid bird's eye view of the glen!" Elise exclaimed. Then her eyes followed the glen north and saw what appeared to be the open sea in the distance. She turned to Jason, her eyebrows raised in query.

"Yes, from this vantage point there's a birds-eye view of the northern shore of Skye and a couple of smaller islands," he said, grinning broadly. "We'll also see them from ground level when we drive north up the A87 coast road."

"I must be on the lookout tomorrow," Elise replied, "but now let's get to the summit."

"By the time we get to the top we'll have climbed over 550m in about one and a half miles. That's not bad going!" Jason volunteered.

......

Soon they were standing beside the cairn that marked the summit. From this vantage point the view north was no longer partly obscured. The southern end of Raasay and the smaller island of Scalpay were now completely visible. Rotating clockwise, they could follow the coast of the Scottish mainland down to the Skye Bridge and on to Skye itself. Elise gripped Jason's hand tight in her delight at such a splendid panorama.

Then they rotated back anti-clockwise past the enticing peaks in the west and, finally, south where the complete outline of Loch Slapin lay map-like below them, its mouth seemingly pointing across the water to another land mass.

"Is that the mainland again?" Elise asked.

"No, it must be the large peninsular that forms the southern extremity of Skye. We could go back to Fort William that way; in fact, it's the shorter route. There's a ferry from Armadale to Mallaig on the mainland and then a very scenic road from there to Fort William."

"Let's not talk about going back yet. I'm enjoying every minute of the present," she whispered. Then she looked up at Jason and added, very shyly: "I'm also enjoying being with you."

Jason's heart leapt. "It's exactly the same for me. You've made these few days so much better than they would have been on my own. I'm so thankful I met you in your time of need and was able to do something to help," he said, trying to restrain his deeper feelings. Then more words tumbled out before he could stop them: "I've never had much success with girls but you're altogether different. I had no idea someone like you could possibly exist and I've fallen in love with you!"

He stopped, appalled at being so impetuous and tactless: Elise must still be feeling the pain of her recent loss and betrayal.

However, after a moment of total surprise, she gave him a wonderful smile and reached up to kiss his cheek. "I'm in love with you and this time I'm sure it's the real thing. But can you really forgive me for my torrid affair with David?"

In reply, Jason took her in his arms and kissed her tenderly. "I love you for who you are. The past is not for me to forgive," he whispered, and, for a few precious moments, they were lost to everything around them.

It was only when they were sharing their simple lunch, gazing out over the sea that Jason spoke again, choosing his words with great care.

"My mother would probably say that our family are Christians because we go to church on rare occasions – Christmas etc. – and I was sent to junior church as a boy, mainly, I guess, because my parents wanted some time to themselves on Sundays, but it would be more accurate to describe myself as an agnostic. Now, however, after finding those bible verses, my agnosticism has been severely shaken. It all stems from what happened to you in Tyndrum. The odds against being presented with the word "peace" in such unusual ways three times in as many days must be enormous. The only reasonable conclusion is that they are intended to help you and need to be taken seriously.

"The basic message of the first bible verse, discovered on yesterday's hike, is that peace is given by Jesus. The second one on the church notice-board goes further. As I remember, it said something like: "Now that we have been put right with God through faith, we have peace with God through our Lord Jesus Christ..." It appears, therefore, that we're being told that Jesus is the key and that human beings can be "put right" with God through him.

"I said a few minutes ago that your past is not mine to forgive, but, from what you told me yesterday, you feel the need to be forgiven and be at peace with your past. Apart from your parents, who will surely understand and forgive, from the Christian point of view it's clearly the forgiveness of God you need. In fact, I'm sure I've got things in my past that need to be forgiven. All this requires faith on our part. The question is how do we get that faith? So perhaps we need to keep our eyes peeled for more clues!"

Elise looked at him, her eyes shining. "Thank you for helping to clarify things. I know I'm all excited about finding you, but there's also something else; somehow I feel we're on the verge of discovering something special!"

Jason reached over and hugged her.

......

The descent did not take as long as the outward journey and the young couple stopped briefly to share a pot of tea and slice of cake in the Blue Shed café.

"We've got to continue running back towards Broadford for about one and a half miles to the point at which a narrow track on the right-hand side doubles back slightly before winding its way down to Loch Slapin," Jason said as he finished his tea. "We then go south, roughly parallel to the shore, climbing gently to about 100m. There should be a good view north towards the head of the loch and the mountains and hills beyond."

"Splendid; I look forward to getting off the road again and running on country tracks," Elise said, giving him such a loving smile that his heart continued to sing all the way to the turning-off point and beyond.

......

The view was just as good as Jason had promised and Elise was almost certain she could pick out Beinn na Cro: the special hill that would always carry happy memories.

They carried on for another two miles, now on a modest descent, before passing a few ruins and a stone barn with a rusty metal roof that had clearly been in more recent use. Here Jason called a water stop.

"I think the earlier ruins mark one of the two hamlets we'll pass this afternoon," he said. "The website says that they were cleared as part of the Highland clearances of 1853!"

Elise sighed. "I remember something about it in our school history lessons. It was not a sudden event but the culmination of things that had occurred over a period of about 200 years, made even worse by the potato blight that had arrived from Ireland not long before. In the end, some landowners were desperate to make the land profitable by introducing sheep farming and the wealthier ones just wanted the land for hunting etc. A lot of poor and desperate people emigrated to Australia and Canada. The landlords sometimes paid their fare just to get rid of them!"

After such unhappy thoughts about the past, the young couple moved on, eventually joining a narrow rough path that ran along a steep slope overlooking the water before dropping down to the shore.

"We've turned east; this is now Loch Eishort," Jason called from behind.

Elise waved her hand in acknowledgement; she was busy winding her way past a jumble of rocks that had fallen from the low cliffs that fringed the water.

They threaded their way carefully on past several waterfalls until the higher ground eventually retreated for a short distance, leaving a sheltered area of gently sloping land only a few metres above sea level. Here were the sad ruins of another village. It was such a sheltered and attractive spot that Elise stopped beside the remains of what had once been a surprisingly well constructed house of grey stone and reached for her water flask.

"It's beautiful and sad at the same time," she sighed. "It must have been terrible to have been uprooted from such a nice place, even though life would have been very hard."

"Especially in a bad year with poor crops," Jason agreed. "It's not as if they could have bought in much from outside because they would have had nothing to trade with."

"Hopefully, they managed to catch fish," Elise surmised as her companion led her up a path running inland and northeast.

The energetic young couple soon left the village far behind as they climbed a steep ridge. A narrow valley with a stream lay some distance below them to the right. Soon they reached a gate, beyond which the path widened into a good track that took them up on to a stretch of almost level ground and then to a cairn marking the summit of the pass.

"We've climbed a good 150m," Jason said, smiling at Elise as they shared more water. She still looked fit and ready for anything. "How I love you!" he thought and then remembered that he no longer had to conceal his feelings and so spoke the words aloud.

There was delight in her eyes as she grabbed hold of him and kissed him hard. For a few minutes they clung together before turning to gaze at the range of mountains now visible in the north from their new vantage point. The only disappointment was the sight of threatening clouds that were gathering in the same direction.

"We'd better hurry on. I've only brought our thin waterproof anoraks and we could get caught in a downpour as bad as on the journey here!" Jason said. "By the way, we'll soon be passing an old marble quarry and join the remains of a railway line built to take the marble down to Broadford."

......

The rain started soon after passing the remains of the quarry, drizzle at first but steadily increasing in intensity. They ran steadily on towards Broadford down the old railway, now devoid of track. The surface made for easier running and Jason's earlier dismay at the rain was totally dispelled when he heard the girl beside him give a cry of sheer joy as she sped down the gentle incline.

"Hurrah, for the rain!" he cried between deep breaths. "Who cares about getting wet?"

The route skirted the side of a long hill. Slightly below them and a short distance to the right, they glimpsed a couple of vehicles passing along the B8083.

"From now on the path will twist about a bit but follow the road for over a mile before joining it very close to Broadford," Jason called. Elise turned slightly to grin at him and nod encouragingly.

......

It was a very wet but happy couple who arrived back at the camper van in the early evening. Sharing an umbrella that Jason found in one of the storage lockers, they hurried to the shower block, endeavouring to keep their changes of clothes dry.

Jason cooked supper while Elise stayed on to put their rather grubby and very wet clothes through a short wash cycle in the machine provided, transferring them to the tumble dryer before she returned to the van for the meal.

"You're a very good cook," she congratulated him, although, on reflection, it was not the quality of the meal that made it special but her inward happiness at what had transpired that day.

That night, they woke occasionally to the sound of heavy rain drumming on the roof of the van. Fortunately it had eased by the following morning but was still drizzling slightly.

"Never mind, we've enjoyed sunshine for most of our outings," Elise remarked.

Chapter 8: Northward Bound

Around 10 am, after stocking up with food at the large Coop store in Broadford, Jason and Elise drove north up the A87 coast road to Portree, the main town on Skye, a journey of about 25 miles. They had anticipated good sea views but, even on the landward side, the hills and mountains displayed a sombre beauty under the dull sky.

After a few miles, the road ahead curved sharply to the left and Jason slowed. "I think we're about to catch a glimpse of the two islands north of Skye that you saw from the top of Beinn na Cro yesterday," he said.

"I was keen to see them at sea level," Elise replied, straining to look across from the passenger seat. "But I must say the bird's eye view was much better!"

The road followed the shore of Loch Ainort inland, and, as the camper rounded the head of the loch, the young couple found themselves in a small valley surrounded by low hills. A turbulent stream cascaded down the slope towards them, passed under the road and hurried on to reach the sea.

"May we stop to look?" Lucy asked. "I love waterfalls and fast running water."

Jason parked in a convenient lay-by. Although it was still spotting with rain, Elise did not seem to notice; full of anticipation, she bounced back along the road and threaded her way along a makeshift path to take a closer look.

It would have been a splendid spot on a sunny day, but, even now, under a lowering sky, it retained a strange attraction. "It must be because Elise is with me," Jason thought as he followed her eager steps. She seemed to sense his feelings because she turned her head to look at him and smile.

......

They drove the remaining 16 miles to Portree in happy companionship and, almost more by luck than judgement, left the main road at the correct junction and found themselves beside what was obviously the town-centre car park.

"Coffee is a top priority," Jason said as he squeezed the camper into a parking bay. "After a quick look at the town, we need to join the A855 coast road to small place called Staffin where I've booked three nights at the caravan site."

"Actually, we joined the A855 when you turned off to get into the town centre; I noticed the road sign," Elise said helpfully. "So we just need to continue the way we were going."

"Thanks for being so observant," Jason grinned at her. "I'll just get a ticket for one hour because we need to move on fairly soon. Not only is it still some distance from here but there's a treat waiting for us after about six miles if the weather improves."

Intrigued, Elise raised her eyebrows in query, but Jason just smiled and shook his head. "It's a surprise. All I will say is that it involves a hike of nearly three miles and a climb of about 280m."

Elise gave a happy laugh. "Just what's needed after a lengthy drive!"

......

They found a café for coffee before briefly exploring the town centre; in fact it was such a pleasant place that they were almost sorry to move on. All the while, Elise had been keeping her eye open for a church or chapel with a notice-board that might offer another clue in their search. As they drove out of the town, she explained what she had been doing.

"Sorry, I completely forgot!" Jason confessed. He did not add that he had been too absorbed with the pleasure of being with her.

The road was taking them north again but it was only after passing two sizable lochs on the right-hand side that the sea came into view again. Almost immediately, Jason turned the campervan off the road and into a small car park.

"We're here," he said. "Today's treat; a three-mile circular scramble to see the Old Man of Storr, a tall pinnacle of rock in a group of several that form a most unusual outcrop on the hilltop."

He paid the parking charge and Elise took his hand as they read some details about the popular tourist spot on a notice-board attached to a stone cairn at the entrance. A family with two young children followed them through the gate on to a well-constructed path. Elise gave the two youngsters a conspiratorial wink before striding ahead with Jason who was consulting the Walk Highlands website on his smartphone.

"The first section is on this excellent path and will make for easy running even when it gets steeper," he reported. "We must be careful to bear right at a couple of forks until we reach another gate opening on to a grassy slope where the going will get much harder and we may be reduced to a scramble."

"Splendid!" Elise murmured, almost gleefully.

Jason grinned at her before continuing. "There'll be good views back over the sea and ahead when the outcrop comes in sight. Some distance above the second gate, there's another junction where we need to go left and follow an indistinct path that loops around the rocks. Anyway, let's get going. You lead."

His companion needed no further encouragement and moved off with the wonderfully smooth springy step that he had admired the day before. She had obviously been well trained in the most efficient long-distance running style where endurance is essential. He recalled his own training and how the instructor had drilled into them the essential elements of proper pacing. He could almost remember the man's exact words.

"Let your foot hit the ground lightly – landing between heel and mid-foot – and then roll quickly forward; keep your ankle flexed to create more force for the push-off; roll onto your toes and spring off the ground; make your calf muscles propel you forward. DON'T let your feet slap the ground. Good running is springy and quiet."

How often the last few words had been shouted at Jason until he had mastered the technique. Now he was being given an almost perfect visual display by the amazing girl now leading him forward and appearing almost oblivious to the increasing incline.

At their first water stop, they turned to gaze back the way they had come. It was well worth it. The road was out of sight, but, clearly visible under a dull sky, lay the lochs they had recently driven past and, beyond them, the sea and the long tapered island of Raasay with the faint outline of the mainland behind.

"Certainly a view to savour," Elise said. Then she spun round and looked ahead. "Those rocks promise to be something spectacular!"

They continued on up the path before descending into a shallow dip and through another gate. Here the path narrowed and rapidly deteriorated before beginning to climb a steep grassy slope scattered with large rocks that had probably fallen from the crags now rising almost menacingly above them. Some smaller rocks had been set in the soil to give climbers a foothold and their progress was reduced to an energetic scramble.

"Turn left here," Jason called from behind. "This must be the beginning of the path that loops around the outcrop."

Although not surprising after all the recent rain, the slope was extremely moist. After a short distance, the winding path became so steep that it would have been near impossible, even in stout trainers, without the stone steps that now formed an almost complete staircase.

Pausing for a breather, the view back towards the sea was stunning. However, an even greater surprise lay in store when they glanced forward and up: the Old Man now surged skywards from a rocky outcrop not far above their heads

The pinnacle was certainly impressive; 50m high, it stood a short distance from its fellows and seemed to be pointing accusingly up as if asking some unknown deity: "Why have I been separated from my companions?"

The young couple climbed on and the path took them slightly to the right of the Old Man before cresting the ridge on which it stood and dropping down the other side. They were now surrounded by massive broken cliffs and pinnacles. One, in particular, looked most unusual: there was a large window-like hole near its top and a much smaller one beside it.

"This one's called the Cathedral for obvious reasons," Jason said as they stopped to gaze, along with two other people who were busy taking photographs. Elise reached for her smartphone to take a quick snap.

"Thank you for all this," she murmured, so gratefully that her companion's heart missed a beat.

Reluctant to leave this strangely atmospheric place, they continued the descent and eventually followed one of a choice of paths going downhill towards the sea. It was not long before they emerged on the path leading back to the parking area.

Jason looked quite surprised. "I think we may have missed a slightly longer detour," he said apologetically.

"Never mind; it's all been splendid!" Elise said as they strode down, no longer wanting to run but just enjoying being together.

......

After following the coast road for another six miles, Elise spotted a small hotel. "May we stop here?" she asked. "I'll treat you to a pot of tea or something." She was quite thirsty by this time – it was late afternoon – and also needed to pay a visit.

"Thanks; that's a nice idea," Jason said, turning off the road to join the few parked cars.

......

When they set off again, Jason remarked: "We've only about four miles to go. The caravan park is just south of Staffin and the access road is on the right-hand side, so keep your eyes peeled for some sort of signpost."

The caravan site turned out to be smaller than the one in Broadford, but had all the basic facilities and their allotted parking lot was in a good position. The whole site was on a slight slope on the seaward side of the main road and the water was just visible through the conifer trees.

After a simple meal, almost entirely prepared by Elise who was now quite familiar with cooking in a very confined space, they walked north into Staffin to find a drink. To their surprise, however, the village, although much smaller than Broadford, was spread out almost randomly in exactly the same way.

In the end, after walking over half a mile, they gave up hope of finding a pub or inn and hopefully approached a restaurant at the far end of a large building advertising itself as the Staffin Stores.

"At least the restaurant's still open," Elise said, noting three cars outside and the welcome notice announcing that food was served all day.

They were greeted by a rather tired-looking waitress behind the service counter. "I'm sorry, the kitchen will soon be closing and we can't take any more orders for hot food," she said.

"No, we had a meal at the caravan site. We were really looking for a drink but there doesn't seem to be a pub in the village," Jason replied.

While he spoke, Elise had been reading the list of the ice-cream deserts available. "Look, they've got banana split – my favourite! Would you like one?"

So they forgot about an alcoholic beverage and settled on banana splits accompanied by coffee.

"But there's no need for you to pay for them," Jason objected when his companion got her purse out and laid it on the table.

"Yes there is!" she insisted. "Look at all the money I'm saving on accommodation. I'm determined to pay for most of our food."

The ice-cream concoctions made a nice change from their normal fare and it was pleasant sitting in the spacious comfort of an almost empty restaurant. However, the waitress was clearly anxious to close and so they hurriedly finished when the last of the other guests departed.

Elise went to the counter to pay the bill that had been left on the table when their food was served, leaving Jason to put the chairs tidily in place and collect their anoraks. As he did so, he spotted something lying under the table. It turned out to be a small leaflet consisting of a single sheet of paper folded neatly in half. But it was what was written on the pale blue cover that really caught his attention.

"JESUS IS PEACE....for those far and near", it proclaimed boldly. Thrusting the leaflet into his pocket, he hurried to join Elise in thanking the waitress, who was now at the entrance waiting to lock up.

Somewhat to Elise's disappointment, they returned to the caravan park even quicker than they had come; she had been hoping to exchange a kiss or two on the way.

"I've got something to show you when we get back," was all Jason would say in response to her unasked question.

Chapter 9: More Revealed

Back in the camper, Jason produced the leaflet from his pocket. "This was under our table," he said. "It has probably been there all day judging by the number of scuff marks on it. Look at the title!"

He sat down beside Elise as she eagerly unfolded the flimsy paper. Even when opened out flat it was only about the size of a large postcard. At the top was a quotation from the New Testament, clearly intended to back up the declaration on the cover.

"But now in Christ Jesus you who were once far off have been brought near by the blood of Christ. For he is our Peace... (Ephesians 2:13-14a)".

This was followed by four short paragraphs highlighted as bullet points:

• Most human beings are searching for something – a better job, more money, a partner, etc. – but, at a deeper level, we are all seeking something else. About 1600 years ago, St Augustine summed it up: "Thou hast made us for thyself, O Lord, and our heart is restless until it finds its rest in thee."

• Because God loves us, he has made a way for us to come to him. That way is through the death of Jesus on the Cross; the sinless one died on behalf of sinners. Jesus said: "I am the way and the truth and the life. No one comes to the Father except through me," (John 14:6).

• Jesus also said on another occasion: "No one can come to me unless the Father who sent me draws him," (John 6:44). Each one of us needs to ask God to reveal the truth about Jesus, because "there is no other name under heaven given to men by which we must be saved," (Acts 4:12).

• Each person, therefore, needs to acknowledge that they are sinful, thank Jesus for dying for them and ask him to be their Saviour, for "if you confess with your mouth, "Jesus is

Lord," and believe in your heart that God raised him from the dead, you will be saved," (Romans 10:9).

Elise looked at her companion, her eyes shining. "This is the final clue!" she declared.

Jason was not quite so sure. His eyes felt tired and he would need to read the small print again in daylight. "How can you be so sure that this is the final one?" he asked.

"Because it gathers up the message of the first two clues and explains what needs to be done. May we go to some quiet spot tomorrow? I feel the need to be alone and uninterrupted."

"Of course we may," Jason assured her. He was more than willing to do whatever it took to help the girl he loved find the peace she had been seeking since that terrible morning in Tyndrum. He was also intrigued by this search for God and becoming increasingly aware that he needed something similar.

After a moment's thought, he continued: "I was going to suggest an outing to the spectacular rock formation at Quiraing tomorrow, but a visit to Fingal's Pinnacles a little further north should suit your purpose better; the website says the place is similar to Storr but less popular and it should be easy to find somewhere really isolated well off the path. Apparently, Fingal was a giant warrior in Scottish mythology and there's a massive cliff there said to be his tomb."

"Thank you for doing so much careful planning; Fingal it is then!" she replied, folding the paper and putting it away safely. She said nothing else as they prepared for bed but the grateful look she gave him spoke volumes.

......

Elise was woken the following morning by a beam of sunlight that had penetrated a narrow gap in the curtains and was falling across her face. She got up quietly, trying not to disturb Jason and peered outside. To her disappointment, the sky was still generally cloudy and the dull ground was only being touched by a few shafts of sunlight. It was, however, dry and the clouds did not appear to be harbouring rain.

She quietly dressed and left the van to visit the washroom, returning a few minutes later to find Jason also up and about. "I'll get some breakfast and begin making sandwiches while you pay a call," she said, placing a good-morning kiss on his bristly cheek.

Jason returned the kiss with a hug, plugged in his razor to charge the battery and disappeared.

......

To make the day's outing more active, the young couple decided to run up the coast road for four miles to the starting point of the Fingal circuit: a small parking area beside the remains of a quarry just south of the hamlet of Flodigarry.

"We'll need to make frequent use of the verge, especially further north when the road narrows to a single track with passing bays," Jason warned his eager companion. "There's not much in Flodigarry apart from an expensive country-house hotel, so we certainly need to take refreshments with us!"

Fortunately the traffic was light at that time of day and, given Elise's enthusiasm, they reached the small car park in about 45 minutes. To their delight, there was only one car. They paused for a quick drink of water and stood looking out across the road. Not far away, the sea could be seen between gaps in the undulating ground flanking the narrow carriageway.

After jogging up the path and getting clear of the face of the old quarry, they skirted the northern shore of a modest stretch of water. "This is Loch Langaig," Jason called from behind.

By now it was clear that some stiff climbing lay ahead; large rocks reared their bulk from a grassy ridge not far away, backed by the huge cliff that Jason had mentioned the previous evening.

Elise let out a whoop of sheer pleasure at the sight. "We're in for a splendid day, despite the dull sky," she predicted and she was to be proved right.

......

After they had passed a second small loch, the path began to climb more steeply for a second time and the view seaward became really impressive. Eventually, they reached more level ground and saw a massive buttress of rock not far to the right.

"That's the end of the cliff – the so-called Fingal's tomb that we saw earlier," Jason explained, now pointing. "The website says there's an indistinct path on our right leading up to a gap or saddle between the buttress and those curious pinnacles of rock. Anyway, we must leave the path we're on at the moment because it carries on southwest to the Quiraing."

Elise's sharp eyes soon spotted the narrow path and eagerly led the way until they reached the brow of the gap. The rear of the buttress now towered up beside them.

They stopped for some water and gazed around them. Visibility had improved and, to their delight, the view towards the Quiraing was very dramatic and just as splendid as the seascapes. Continuing over the saddle, they found themselves in a rather boggy hollow. The indistinct route then descended the slope and entailed climbing over a fence followed by a dry-stone wall before the strange cluster of Fingal's pinnacles could be seen not far below with the sea beyond.

The rock formations were smaller than those at Storr and more closely grouped. With the seascape as background, they were oddly reminiscent of a series of grey sandcastles in varying stages of collapse and recently abandoned by giant children. Even better, as far as Elise was concerned, the place was almost deserted; this was the ideal opportunity for the time of reflection she had promised herself.

"Let's find a remote spot down there where we can be quiet," she said, with an increasing sense of anticipation.

......

Jason spread out their waterproof anoraks in a secluded spot not far from one of the smaller pinnacles and well away from the path. They both had records of the biblical clues on their smart-phones and so it was only necessary for Jo to read aloud from the leaflet found the previous evening before they could sit in quiet reflection.

Jason found himself being pulled two directions. Although he desperately wanted the girl he loved to find release from her inner pain, he still found it difficult, as a hard-headed astrophysicist, to accept the truth of all that had appeared almost miraculously over the last few days. On the other hand, if there was some all-powerful Being behind everything that exists, then it was entirely possible for such a Being to choose to do things in a certain way. Perhaps Jo and he were being shown that way.

But where were the facts? Wait a minute! Why was he so intent on demanding facts? This was by no means always the case in science. For example, there was a strong belief in the so-called Big Bang – the phenomenally fast expansion of all the energy and matter in the universe from an ill-defined singularity. However, the Big Bang is only a theory deduced from the observations of the universe and mathematical analysis that have taken place over the last two hundred years or so. In contrast, it is an excepted scientific fact, thanks to the brilliance of Einstein, that energy and matter are interchangeable, given the right circumstances. But where did they originate, energy in particular?

So why then did he, a (hopefully) budding scientist, have difficulty in accepting the possibility that the source of all energy is an infinitely powerful deity, even the God written about in the Bible? If the latter is true, then that God is not only all powerful but also the source of a love so deep and all embracing that it reaches out to draw human beings into relationship – if they are willing! What if the biblical clues and other information provided so unexpectedly are that love in action? If so, then Jesus seems to be the key.

Jason's almost fevered thoughts fell silent and he sat stock still with his eyes staring at nothing in particular.

Suddenly, without warning and in less time than it took to blink, he was immersed in what he could only describe later as a "glory" more real than anything around him. The experience only lasted a fleeting moment but left him with the total certainty – far above mere knowledge – that Almighty God was offering to be his Father and that Jesus was indeed the way to Him.

"Wow!" Jason exclaimed, turning to Jo in awe and excitement, "I am now a believer!"

Elise's eyes were full of tears. "So am I!" she responded. "In fact, I have just asked Jesus to be my Saviour! I was suddenly filled with so much love that I almost burst. A hardness of some sort seemed to melt inside me and I knew without a shadow of doubt that Jesus loves me, that he died for the sin of the world and now lives to intercede for us.

"Some of my long-forgotten childhood memories of attending church with my parents and our family prayers came flooding back and made sense to me for the first time. I found myself whispering: "Jesus, please forgive my past and make me the person you want me to be." And it happened! I feel completely clean inside!"

"I'm so glad!" Jason exclaimed. "I want to do the same, but I've never prayed from the heart before. Can you help me?"

Elise smiled. "Just repeat after me ...," she said, and he did.

Full of wonder at what had happened, they sat for several minutes basking in the atmosphere that surrounded them until it faded. Then, gathering up their belongings, they made their way back to the main path. Fingal's pinnacles would always remain a very special place.

Chapter 10: The Quiraing and Beyond

Once back on the main path, Elise turned left as if making for the coast road up which they had come from Staffin, but Jason stopped her.

"I've just realized we're on part of the Skye Trail," he said. "This long section runs down from Flodigarry, past the Quiraing and on through the centre of Skye to reach the coast near Storr. We can get back to the camping site by going south as far as the road going east to Staffin – the one we would have taken if we had been aiming for the Quiraing this morning."

"Brilliant! I'm so happy I could run for miles!" Elise exclaimed, as she turned and led off joyfully.

The path climbed slowly towards the massive outcrops they had spied earlier from the higher ground and came to a junction where the path bore left and ran below the Quiraing's dramatic line of crags. The latter rose about 200m above them and the views were magnificent: to the east the sea and to the south a long ridge disappearing into the far distance.

"That ridge forms the spine of Skye and starts just north of Flodigarry. In fact, we're running along its flank now," Jason explained as they paused for water. "Most of the peaks are less than 500m. Perhaps tomorrow we could go back to Storr and explore the other end of this section of the Trail."

"Sounds good to me!" Elise said.

They continued up the gentle gradient to the heart of the Quiraing, encountering more and more visitors who had walked up from the car park. And no wonder: the views were amongst the best the young couple had seen so far and Jason was so impressed that he called Elise to stop for a moment. He had also just spotted a curious group of three spiky crags.

"Those are called "The Prism" apparently," he said.

All too soon, they were descending a path that contoured the slope, crossed a deep rocky gully, and came out on the Uig to Staffin road. Here, to give Elise a rest, Jason took over the lead, ready to mount the verge whenever the traffic required.

They would have plenty to discuss over the evening meal in the campervan, but, for now, still buoyed up by the wonderful events of the last hour or so, they simply let thoughts meander seemingly at random through their minds.

Jason knew with absolute certainty that the commitment he had just made with Elise's help had been honest and not done merely to please the girl he loved with all his heart. He had been deeply stirred by the scripture verses that had appeared, almost miraculously, across their path. However, he realized that these clues had made even more of an impact on Elise, due in part to her early religious background and even more to the great burden of guilt and sorrow she had carried so impetuously up the West Highland Way with scant regard for her safety.

So it was that he ran on towards Staffin with a deep thankfulness and wonderful excitement flooding his whole being.

......

Meanwhile, Elise's feet floated almost effortlessly over the surface of the road, such was her joy and gratitude to Jesus for rescuing her from the depth of her anguish in the Tyndrum café – without which she might have done something completely unthinkable. Jesus had then gently led her and Jason into a new relationship with God in which the guilt and shortcomings of the past had been wiped out through the Cross. She seemed to know with total certainty – how, she had no idea – that all the shame and old broken things had passed away and she was now a completely new creation. Oh the joy of it! And it was in the wonderful company of the man she loved!

The End

Printed and bound by CPI Group (UK) Ltd, Croydon, CR0 4YY
22/03/2024
03748919-0004